"Couldn't you be released from the spell?" the sister cried.
(*The Six Swans*, page 160)

GRIMM'S
FAIRY TALES

Iain Richard
Alexander

WARD, LOCK & CO., LIMITED
LONDON, MELBOURNE AND CAPE TOWN

1139

PRINTED IN ENGLAND BY THE HOLLEN STREET PRESS LIMITED
SOHO, LONDON W.1

Preface

FOR more than a century the stories so lovingly collected by the Brothers Grimm have been the delight of children, and of others who, whatever their age, will always be children at heart.

Jacob Grimm was born in 1785, his brother Wilhelm a year later. Their father died while they were still lads, and they learnt only too well that " the wolf at the door " may be more than a fable. All through their lives they were the best of friends, living together, and sharing the same studies and hobbies. On leaving school, they became greatly interested in German and Danish folk-lore, and spent much of their time wandering about the country, gleaning from peasants and the simpler townspeople a rich harvest of legends, which they would write down as nearly as possible in the words in which they were told. The first collection was published in 1812 ; other stories were gradually added, until there were more than two hundred. Some, it may be noted, are found in various forms in many languages, and have doubtless come to us from a period long before there were any books at all.

This selection comprises most of the more popular stories, especially those suitable for younger children. Complete editions can be obtained from the same publishers.

H. G.

CONTENTS

The Frog Prince

In the good old times, when wishes often came true, there lived a King whose daughters were all beautiful, but the youngest was so beautiful that the sun himself, who had seen so much beauty, wondered at her every time he kissed her face.

Close to the King's castle was a dark forest, and in the forest under an old lime tree was a well; here on warm days the royal child used to come and sit on the bank by the cool water. When she was dull she took a golden ball, threw it in the air and caught it again, and that was her favourite amusement.

It happened once that the Princess's golden ball, instead of falling into the little hands she held out to catch it, rolled along the ground into the water. The child followed the ball with her eyes, but it disappeared, and the well was deep, so deep that you couldn't see the bottom. Then she began to cry, and cried louder and louder, as if nothing could comfort her; and as she wailed someone called out, "Why, Princess, what's the matter? You cry loudly enough to move a stone to pity." She looked round to see where the voice came from, and beheld a frog poking his fat, ugly head out of the water.

"Ah! is it you, old water-splasher?" she said. "I am crying because my golden ball has fallen into the well."

"Well, don't cry any more," answered the frog. "I can help you. What will you give me if I fetch your toy for you?"

"Anything you like to ask for, dear frog," she said: "my clothes, my pearls and precious stones, or even the gold coronet I wear."

The frog answered:

"Your clothes, your pearls, your precious stones, your gold coronet—I don't want any of them; but if you'll

7

love me and let me be your chum and playmate, sit by you at table, eat off your little gold plate, drink out of your little goblet, and sleep in your little bed; if you'll promise all this, I'll dive down and get your golden ball."

"Very well," she said. "I'll promise anything you like if you'll only bring back my ball." She thought to herself, "What nonsense the foolish frog talks! He can only sit in the water and croak to other frogs, and can't be the chum of any human being."

So the frog ducked his head and sank. In a little while he rose to the surface with the ball in his mouth, and threw it on the grass. The Princess was so delighted at seeing her pretty plaything again that she picked it up and ran off.

"Stop! stop!" shouted the frog; "take me with you; I can't run so fast."

But it was no use; croak as loud as he would, she took no notice and ran home, where she soon forgot all about the poor frog, who was obliged to descend into his well again.

The next day, when the Princess had just sat down to table with the King and all the court, and was eating off her little gold plate, *splish*, *splash*, *splish*, *splash* was heard, and something hopped up the marble stairs, knocked at the door, and called, "Youngest Princess, let me in!" She ran to the door to see who was outside, and as she opened it saw the frog seated there. She slammed the door violently, and hurried back to her place in a great fright. The King observed that her heart was beating quickly, and said:

"Child, why are you frightened? Is there a giant at the door come to carry you off?"

"Oh, no," she answered, "it isn't a giant, but a nasty frog."

"What does the frog want with you?"

"Oh, dear father, yesterday, when I was in the forest playing by the well my golden ball fell into the water. And because I cried so, the frog fetched it for me, and because he asked me, I promised he should be my companion, but I never thought he could come so far out of his water. Now he is outside, and wants to come in here."

Meanwhile there was another knock at the door, and a voice called :

> " Open the door, my Princess, dear,
> Open the door to thy true love here !
> Remember the promise you yesterday made
> By the deep well cool in the lime tree's shade."

Then the King said, " You must not break your promise, so go and let him in."

She went and opened the door, and the frog hopped in, followed her to her chair, and called out, " Lift me up to you."

She shuddered, but the King ordered her to do as she was asked. The frog was not content with being on the chair, and wanted to get on to the table. When there he said, " Push your little gold plate nearer, so that we may eat together." The Princess did so, but it was easy to see that she did not like it. The frog ate with relish, but she could hardly get down a morsel. At last he said, " I have eaten till I am satisfied. Now I am tired ; take me to your little room, have your silk bed turned down, and we will lie down and go to sleep."

The Princess began to cry at the thought of the cold frog whom she's daren't touch sleeping in her pretty, clean bed.

The King grew angry with her and said, " Those who have helped us in our need are not to be despised afterwards."

So she lifted the frog with two dainty fingers, carried him upstairs, and put him down in a corner. But when she was in bed he crept to the bedside, and said, " I am tired, I want to go to bed too. Lift me up, please, or I'll tell your father." Then she really flew into a passion, took him up, and flung him with all her might against the wall. " Now you can go to sleep if you like, you nasty, ugly frog."

But when he fell to the ground he was not a frog any longer, but a Prince with beautiful smiling eyes, and, according to her father's wishes, he became her dear chum and playmate. He told her how he had been bewitched by a wicked old witch, and no one had the power to release him from the well but the little Princess, and to-morrow they would travel back to his kingdom together. They fell asleep, and when the sun was up the next morning, a carriage with eight white horses drew up at the door. The horses had white plumes nodding on their heads, and gold harness, and behind stood the servant of the young Prince, the faithful Henry, who had been so grieved when his master was turned into a frog that he had put three bands of iron round his heart to prevent its breaking from sorrow and grief.

The carriage was to take the young Prince back to his own kingdom, and the faithful Henry helped in his master and the Princess, and stationed himself behind again. They hadn't gone far before they heard a crack as if something were breaking. Again, and yet again, a crack was heard on the road, and each time the royal couple thought something in the carriage had burst, but it was only the iron bands springing from Henry's heart, because he was so overjoyed at his master's happiness.

Hansel and Grethel

NEAR a large wood once lived a poor woodcutter with his wife and two children. The little boy was called Hänsel and the little girl Grethel. They rarely had nice things to eat, and when there was a famine in the land they could not get so much as their daily bread. As he lay in bed at night the father was greatly troubled ; he sighed and groaned and said to his wife :

" What is to become of us ? How are we to feed our little ones when we haven't anything ourselves ? "

" I tell you what, husband," answered the woman, " to-morrow morning early we will lead the children far into the wood, light them a fire, give each a bit of bread, and then go to our work and leave them alone. They will never find their way home, and we shall be rid of them."

" No, wife," said the man, " I cannot do that ; how could anyone have the heart to leave two dear children alone in the wood to be devoured by wild beasts ? "

" Oh ! " said she, " then we must all four die of hunger." She continued to persuade him, and at last he half consented.

The two children were so hungry that they had not been able to go to sleep, and they had overheard what their step-mother proposed to do with them. Grethel wept bitter tears and said to Hänsel, " It is all up with us."

" Don't cry, Grethel," said Hänsel, " I will see that this doesn't happen."

When the old couple had fallen to sleep, he put on his little coat, crept down and let himself out at the back door. The moon was shining brightly, and the white pebbles on the path in the front of the house shone like new coins. Hänsel stooped and stuffed his coat pockets full of pebbles. Then he went back and said to Grethel, " Be comforted,

little sister, and go to sleep. God will not forsake us ";
and he lay down on his little bed.

When day dawned the woman called the two children
and told them to dress before the sun was high. "Get up,
both of you," she said, "and come into the wood and pick
up sticks." Then she gave each a piece of bread, and told
them to keep it for dinner and not eat it before, as they
would get nothing else. Grethel put the bread under her
apron, because Hänsel's pockets were full of pebbles.

Soon after, they all started together for the wood. They
had not gone far before Hänsel stood still and looked back
at the house. He did this again and again, till his father
said, "Hänsel, what are you gaping at ? "

"Oh, father," said Hänsel, "I am looking at my white
kitten, who is sitting on the roof waving me good-bye."

"That isn't your kitten, silly child," said the woman
" it's the morning sunlight shining on the chimney.
But Hänsel had not been really looking at the kitten ;
he was scattering behind him the pebbles out of his pocket.

When they came to the middle of the wood the father
said, "Now, children, pick up sticks, and we will make a
fire."

Hänsel and Grethel built up quite a pile of twigs,
and when the fire was lighted and the flames were rising
high, the woman said, "You can lie down by the fire
and rest yourselves while we go further to hew wood.
When we have finished we will come and fetch you."

Hänsel and Grethel sat by the fire, and when dinner-
time came, ate their bread, and because they heard the
blows of the hatchet they thought their father was not
far off. But it was not the hatchet they heard, but a
branch that he had tied to a rotten tree, and which the
wind blew up and down. And they sat such a long time
that for very weariness they closed their eyes and went
to sleep. They did not wake till it was night, and pitch
dark. Grethel began to cry and said, "We shall never
find our way out of the wood."

"Wait," said Hänsel : "the moon will be up in a
minute, and then we'll find our way fast enough."

Ere long the great full moon rose in the sky, and Hänsel
took his little sister's hand and followed the track of the

pebbles, which shone like silver coins and showed them the way. They walked the whole night, and at break of day reached their father's house. They knocked at the door, and when the woman opened it and saw Hänsel and Grethel she said, " Why did you sleep so long in the wood ? We began to think you were not coming back at all."

The father was delighted to see the children, for it had gone to his heart to desert them so cruelly.

Not long afterwards there was again distress everywhere, and the children heard their mother saying to their father in the night, " There is hardly anything left to eat, only half a loaf of bread, and when that is gone what are we to do ? The children must be done away with. We will take them deeper into the wood this time, so that they will not be able to find their way out. It's the only thing to be done to save us."

The man's heart was heavy, and he thought, " I would rather share our last crust with the children." But the woman had made up her mind, and all the man said made no difference. When you have said " A " you must say " B " too, and as he had given in the first time he was obliged to give in the second time.

The children, however, had heard the whole of the conversation. When his parents had gone to sleep, Hänsel got up again to go out as he had done before and pick up pebbles, but he found the woman had locked the door. All the same, he comforted his little sister, saying, " Never mind, Grethel, don't cry, but go to sleep. God will take care of us."

At dawn the woman came and roused the children. She gave them each a slice of bread, but it was smaller than last time.

As they walked to the wood Hänsel crumbled the bread in his pocket, stood still now and then, and dropped a crumb on the ground.

" Hänsel, why do you loiter behind and look round ? " his father asked.

" I am looking at my little dove, who is sitting on the roof to coo good-bye."

" Stupid," cried the woman, " it is not your dove, but

the morning sun shining on the chimney." But Hänsel went on dropping his crumbs by the way.

The woman led the children deeper and deeper into the wood, to a part where they never had been before. Again a huge fire was kindled, and their mother said, " Stay here, children, and when you are tired take a nap. We are going further to chop wood. When we have finished we will fetch you."

When dinner-time came Grethel divided her bread with Hänsel, because he had scattered his as they came along. Then they fell asleep, and the evening went by without anyone coming to them. They did not wake till it was pitch dark. Hänsel comforted his sister by saying, " Wait till the moon is up, then we shall see the bread crumbs I strewed on the ground, and that will show us the way home."

But when the moon rose they could see no bread crumbs, for the birds which flew in the woods and fields had picked up every one.

Hänsel said, " We shall soon find our way, Grethel."

But they did not find it—though they walked the whole night and the whole of the next day, they were still in the wood and faint from hunger, for they had eaten nothing but a few berries. And now, because they were so tired and their legs would not carry them farther, they lay down under a tree and fell asleep.

The third morning after they had left their father's house they were still deeper in the wood, and quite lost. If help did not come, they knew they would perish. Then they saw a beautiful snow-white bird sitting on a branch, and it was singing so beautifully that they stopped to listen. It spread its wings when it had finished its song, and flew in front of them, and they followed it till it perched on the roof of a little house which, on coming near, they found was built of bread and thatched with cake, the windows being made of barley-sugar.

" We will set to work," said Hänsel, " and make a good meal for once. I will have a good slice of the roof, and you, Grethel, shall begin with a window, which will taste nice and sweet."

Hänsel climbed up and broke off a bit of the roof, to

see how it tasted, and Grethel stood by a window and nibbled it. Then a voice called from inside :

> " Nibble ! nibble ! nibble !
> Who's nibbling at my house ? "

The children answered :

> " The wind, the wind,
> The child of heaven,"

and ate on, quite unconcerned.

Hänsel, who found that the roof tasted very good, had torn off another great bit, and Grethel had taken out a window-pane and sat down to enjoy it. Suddenly the door opened and an old woman, leaning on a crutch, hobbled out. Hänsel and Grethel shook in their shoes for fright, letting the good stuff fall from their hands.

The old woman nodded her palsied head, and said, " Dear children, who brought you here ? Come in, do, and stay with me ; no harm shall come to you ! "

She took them by the hand and led them into the house. There a good dinner stood ready, milk pancakes, with sugar, apples, and nuts. Afterwards, two little white beds were uncovered, and Hänsel and Grethel lay down in them, and felt as if they were in heaven.

But the old woman was only pretending to be friendly ; she was really a wicked old witch, who lay in wait for children, and had only had her house built of things good to eat in order to lure them into her clutches. When once she had them safe in her power, she slaughtered, cooked, and ate them. The witch had pink eyes and could not see far, but she had keen scent, like animals, and could smell human flesh a long way off. Directly Hänsel and Grethel came near her house, she had laughed, chuckled wickedly, and said to herself, " I'll have them on toast— they shan't escape."

Early the next morning, before the children were awake, she got up, and as she saw their round rosy cheeks, she muttered, " There's a tasty dish." Then she shook Hänsel, and, seizing him with her shrivelled hand, carried him to a little stable, where she shut him in behind a grating. He howled as loudly as he could, but it was no use. Next she went to Grethel, shook her and screamed, "Get up, lazy girl, and go and draw water to cook your brother something good ; he is outside in the stable and must be fattened up ; when he is fat I shall eat him."

Grethel began to cry bitterly, but she was forced to do what the wicked witch commanded.

Hänsel was now given the most nourishing food, but Grethel got only crab-shells. Every morning the old witch hobbled to the stable and cried :

"Hänsel, put your finger out that I may feel how fat you are getting." But Hänsel used to stick out a bone instead of a finger, and the old woman, whose eyes were so dim that she could not see, marvelled that he did not grow fat.

When four weeks had passed, and Hänsel remained still thin, she lost patience and declared she would not wait longer.

"Here, Grethel," she cried to the girl, "make haste and draw water—whether Hänsel is fat or thin, I will kill and eat him to-morrow ! "

The poor little sister wept and lamented as she brought the water, and tears poured down her cheeks ! "Dear God, help us ! " she prayed. "If the wild beasts had eaten us in the woods we should at least have died together."

When the witch had gone poor Grethel watched her chance and ran to Hänsel, telling him what she had heard :

"We must run away quickly, for the old woman is a wicked witch, who will kill us."

But Hänsel said : "I know how to get out, for I have loosened the fastening. But you must first steal her fairy wand, that we may save ourselves if she should follow, and bring, too, the pipe that hangs in her room."

Grethel managed to get both the wand and the pipe, and away the children went.

When the old witch came to see whether her meal was ready, she sprang in a great rage to the window, and, though her eyes were bad, she spied the children running away.

She quickly put on her boots, which went yards at a step, and had scarcely made two steps with them before she overtook the children. But Grethel had seen that she was coming after them, and, by the help of the magic wand, turned Hänsel into a lake of water, and herself into a swan which swam in the middle of it. The witch sat on the shore and tried to decoy the swan by throwing crumbs of bread to it; but it would not come near her, and she was at last forced to go home without her prisoners.

Then Grethel, by means of the wand, changed herself and Hänsel back to their proper forms, and they journeyed on until dawn of day. The girl then turned herself into a beautiful rose in the midst of a quickset hedge; and Hänsel sat by the side.

Soon the witch came striding along.

"Good piper," she said, "may I pluck that beautiful rose?"

"Oh, yes," said he.

She went to the hedge in a hurry to gather the flower —well knowing what it was—and Hänsel pulled out his pipe and began to play.

Now the pipe was a fairy pipe, and whoever heard it was obliged to dance, whether one liked or not. So the old witch was forced to dance a jig, on and on without rest, and could not stop to reach the rose. As Hänsel did not cease playing for a moment the thorns tore the clothes from her body, and pricked her sorely, and at last she stuck quite fast.

Then Grethel set herself free once more, and she and Hänsel set out for home. After travelling a long way, Grethel grew tired, so they laid themselves down to sleep in a hollow tree that grew in a meadow near the wood. As they slept the witch—who had contrived to get out of the prickly bush—came by; and, seeing her wand, was glad to lay hold of it. At once she turned poor Hänsel into a fawn.

When Grethel woke and found what had happened she wept bitterly over the poor creature. The tears rolled from his eyes, as he laid himself beside her.

Grethel said, "Rest in peace, dear fawn; I will never leave you."

She took off her long golden necklace and put it round

his neck, then she plucked some rushes and plaited them into a string, and led the poor fawn by her side wherever she went.

At last one day they came to a little cottage; and Grethel, seeing that it was quite empty, said, "We can live here."

She gathered leaves and moss to make a soft bed for the fawn; and every morning she went out and plucked nuts and berries for herself, and shrubs and tender grass for her friend. The fawn ate out of her hand, and played and frisked about her. In the evening, when Grethel was tired, she laid her head on the fawn and slept; and if only poor Hänsel could have had his right form again they would have led a very happy life.

After living for years in the wood by themselves until Grethel was a grown maiden, it chanced that the King came one day to hunt there. When the fawn heard the echoing of the horns, the baying of the dogs, and the shouts of the huntsmen, he wished very much to see what was going on.

"Oh, sister!" said he, "let me go out into the wood. I can stay no longer."

He begged so long that at last she let him go.

"But," said she, "be sure to come back in the evening. I shall shut the door to keep out the huntsmen, but if you tap and say, 'Sister, let me in,' I shall know you. If you do not speak, I shall keep the door fast."

Then away sprang the fawn, frisking and bounding along in the open air. The King and his huntsmen saw and followed the beautiful creature, but could not over-take him; for just as they thought they were sure of their prize he would spring over the bushes and be out of sight at once.

When it grew dark the fawn came running home to the hut and tapped, saying, "Sister, let me in!" Then Grethel opened the door, and in he jumped, and slept soundly all night on his soft bed.

Next morning the hunt went on; and when he heard the hunstmen's horns the fawn said, "Sister, open the door for me; I must go."

When the King and the hunstmen saw the fawn they

again gave chase. The chase lasted the whole day, but at last the huntsmen surrounded him, and one wounded him in the foot, so that he became lame and could hardly crawl home. The man who had wounded him followed behind and heard the little fawn say, " Sister, let me in," upon which the door opened and shut again. The huntsman went to the King and told him what he had seen and heard and the King said, " To-morrow we will have another chase."

Grethel was very frightened when she saw that her dear fawn was wounded ; but after washing the blood away she put some healing herbs on the place. In the morning there was nothing to be seen of the wound, and when the horn blew the little thing said, " I cannot stay here, I must go and look on ; I will take care they don't catch me."

But Grethel said, " I am sure they will kill you this time : I will not let you go."

" I shall die of grief," said he, " if you keep me here." Then Grethel was forced to let him go : she opened the door with a heavy heart, and he bounded gaily into the wood.

When the King saw the fawn he cried to his men, " Chase him all day long till you catch him ; but let no one do him harm."

At sunset, however, they had not been able to overtake him, and the King called the huntsmen, saying to the one who had watched, " Now show me the little hut."

So they went to the door and tapped, and the King said, " Sister, let me in."

The door was opened, and the King went in, and there stood a maiden more lovely than any he had ever seen.

Grethel was very frightened when she saw that it was not the fawn but a King with a golden crown who had entered her hut, but he spoke kindly and took her hand, and after they had talked awhile, he said, " Will you come with me to my castle and be my wife ? "

" Yes," said Grethel, " I will go to your castle, but I cannot be your wife ; and my fawn must go with me, for I cannot part with him."

" Well," said the King, " he shall come and live with you all your life, and shall want for nothing."

B

Just then in sprang the little fawn, and Grethel tied the string to his neck, and they left the hut together.

Then the King lifted Grethel on to his prancing horse and they rode to his palace, the fawn running behind them. On the way Grethel told the King her story. He knew the old witch and her wicked ways and sent for her, commanding her sternly to change the fawn into human form again.

When she saw her dear brother restored, Grethel was so grateful to the King that she at once consented to marry him. They lived happily all their days, and Hänsel became the King's chief counsellor.

The Fisherman and His Wife

THERE was once a fisherman who lived with his wife in a dirty little hovel close by the sea. The fisherman went every day to fish; and he fished and fished.

One day he sat by his line, looking down into the clear water; and he looked and looked.

Then the line ran out to the bottom of the sea, deep down; and when he hauled it up there was a great carp at the end. And the carp said to him. "Listen, fisherman, I pray you don't kill me. I'm not a carp; I'm an enchanted Prince. Of what use would it be to you to kill me? You would not find my flesh good; put me back in the water and let me swim away."

"Well," said the man, "you needn't make so many words about it; I wouldn't think of keeping a carp that can speak." So saying, he set him down in the clear water; and the carp swam away, leaving a long streak of blood behind him, and the fisherman went back into his hovel to his wife.

"Goodman," said the wife, "have you not caught anything to-day?"

"No," replied he, "that is, I caught a carp, but he said he was an enchanted Prince, so I let him swim away."

"Didn't you wish for anything?" asked the wife.

"No," answered the husband, "what should I wish for?"

"Oh," said the wife, "it's very uncomfortable living in a dirty hovel like ours; you ought to have wished for a pretty little cottage. Go back again and call him; tell him we want a little hut; he'll do that for us, I'm certain."

"But," said the man, "what should I go back there for?"

"Why," said the wife, "you caught him, and you let him swim away. He's sure to do it. Go at once."

The man did not care much to go, but he did not want to cross his wife, so he went off to the sea.

When he came there, the sea was all green and yellow, and not so calm, by a great deal, as it had been. He went and stood on the shore and said:

> "Oh, fish in the sea, pray listen to me,
> For my wife won't let be as I'd have it be."

The carp came swimming up, and said, "What does she want?"

"Oh," said the man, "I caught you just now, and my wife says I ought to have wished for something. She does not like to live in our hovel any longer; she wants a cottage."

"Go home," said the carp, "she has one already."

So the man went home, and his wife was no longer in the hovel; a cottage stood in its place, and she was sitting in front of the door, on a bench. Then his wife took him by the hand and said, "Just come in and look. Is not this much better?"

They went in; and in the cottage there was a little passage, and a pretty little parlour and bedroom, in which their bed stood, and a kitchen and a larder, all of the best kind, with utensils in abundance, tin-ware and brass-ware, and everything that was necessary. And there was also a little yard with chickens and ducks, and a little garden full of vegetables and fruit.

"See," said the wife; "isn't that nice?"

"Yes," answered her husband, "we'll stay here, and live very happily."

"We'll consider about that," said his wife.

So they had their supper and went to bed.

Things went on well enough for a week or a fortnight. Then the wife said, "Listen, husband—this cottage is too small, and both the yard and the garden are too confined; the carp might give us a larger house. I must live in a great stone castle. Go to the carp, and ask him to give us a castle."

"Ah, wife," said the man, "this cottage is quite good enough; what should we want to live in a castle for?"

"Nonsense," replied the wife; "just you go to the carp; he can very well do that."

"No, wife," said the man, "the carp has just given us this cottage; I don't like to go to him again. He might be angry at it."

"Just you go," cried the woman; "he can do it, and he'll do it willingly; just you go."

The man's heart was heavy, and he objected to go; he kept whispering to himself, "It's not right"; but he went for all that.

When he came to the sea-shore the water was dark blue and violet in colour, and grey and thick, and no longer green and yellow; but it was still calm. So he stood by the margin, and said:

> "Oh, fish in the sea, pray listen to me,
> For my wife won't let be as I'd have it be."

"Well, what does she want?" said the carp.

"Oh," said the man, half-frightened, "she wants to live in a stone castle."

"Go home," said the carp; "she's standing before the door now."

So the man went away, thinking to go home. But when he came there he saw a great stone palace, and his wife stood on the steps, about to go in; and she took him by the hand and said, "Do you come in with me."

So he went in with her; and in the palace was a vestibule all inlaid with marble, and there were a number of servants who threw open the great doors, and the walls were all shining and covered with beautiful colours; and in the rooms were gilded chairs and tables in abundance; chandeliers of crystal hung from the ceilings; there were carpets in all the halls and chambers; and the tables were loaded with costly viands and rare things. And behind the house was a great courtyard, with stables, and horses, and cows, and magnificent coaches; and there was a great and beautiful garden, with the most splendid flowers and the rarest fruit trees; and a park more than two miles long, in which were stags, and roes, and hares, and everything a man could wish for.

"Well," said the wife, "isn't this fine?"

"Oh, yes," answered the man, "and it shall remain so. We'll stay in the beautiful castle, and be contented."

"We'll consider the matter," said his wife; "and first we'll sleep upon it." And with that they both went to bed.

The next morning the wife awoke first. It was just day, and from her bed she could see the glorious country lying stretched out before her. Presently her husband began to stir. Then she pushed him in the side with her elbow and said, "Husband, get up, and come with me to the window. See; might we not be rulers over all this country? Go to the carp, and say we want to be rulers."

"Oh, wife!" said the man, "why should we want to be rulers? I don't want to be ruler."

"Well," said the wife, "if you don't want to be, I do. Go to the carp, and say I must be a Sovereign."

"Ah, wife," cried the man, "why should you want to be Sovereign? I can't tell him that."

"And why not?" retorted the woman. "Just you go at once, for I must be Sovereign."

The man went away, and was quite concerned because his wife wanted to be ruler. "That's not right; I'm sure it's not right," thought the man; and he determined not to go; but he went after all.

And when he came to the sea it was of a dark grey colour, and turbid, and was fermenting from below and exhaled quite a nasty odour. He stood by the shore and said:

> "Oh, fish in the sea, pray listen to me,
> For my wife won't let be as I'd have it be."

"What does she want?" asked the carp.

"Oh," said the man, "she wants to be ruler."

"Go home with you," said the carp, "she has her wish."

The man went home. And when he came near the

castle, he saw that it had grown much larger; and there was a great tower to it, with beautiful sculpture; and a sentry stood before the gate, and there were a great number of soldiers, and a band, with drums and trumpets. And when he came into the palace, everything was of pure marble and gold; velvet covers to the chairs and tables, with great gold tassels. Then the doors of the hall flew open, and showed the whole splendour of a court; and his wife was sitting on a lofty throne of gold and diamonds, and had a great golden crown on her head, and in her hand a sceptre of pure gold and precious stones. On each side of the throne stood six maids of honour, all in a row, and each of them was a head shorter than her neighbour. Then he went up to her and said, " Well, wife, so you're ruler now ? "

" Yes," she answered, " I'm ruler now."

He stood for a time looking at her, then said, " Ah, wife, how capital it is, that you're a monarch; now we won't wish for anything more."

"Not at all, husband," answered the wife, and she became quite agitated. " I'm getting tired of this, and can't bear it any longer. Go to the carp and say I should like to be Emperor."

" Oh, wife," said the man, " why do you want to be Emperor ? "

"Husband," said she, " go to the carp. I will be Emperor."

" But, wife," cried he, " the carp can't make you an Emperor, and I don't like to speak to him about it. There's only one Emperor in the empire; the carp can't make an Emperor, indeed he can't."

" What ! " cried the woman. " I'm a ruler, and you're only my husband; will you be off directly ? Go at once; if he can make me a ruler he can make me an Emperor too; and I absolutely will be Emperor. Go directly."

He was obliged to go. But as he went, he felt quite afraid, and as he walked on he thought, " This is sure not to end well. To be an Emperor ! It's too impertinent, and the carp will be tired at last."

Thinking thus, he came to the sea. But the sea was quite black and thick, and it boiled up from below, so that the bubbles burst on the surface, and the wind ruffled it, and raised large waves, and the man felt afraid. But he stood by the shore and said :

> "Oh, fish in the sea, pray listen to me,
> For my wife won't let be as I'd have it be."

"What does she want ? " asked the carp.

"Alas," answered the man, "my wife wants to be Emperor."

"Go home," replied the carp, "she is Emperor already."

So the man went back ; and when he got home all the palace was of polished marble, with alabaster statues and gold decoration. Before the gate soldiers were marching to the braying of trumpets and the beating of drums and cymbals ; and inside the palace barons and counts were walking up and down, just as servants ; they opened the doors, which were of pure gold, to him. And when he had gone in he saw his wife sitting on a throne made of one single piece of gold, thousands of feet high ; she had a great golden crown on, three yards high, and set round with brilliants and carbuncles; in one hand she held the sceptre, in the other the orb ; and in two rows each side of her stood her guards, each man smaller than his neighbour, from the greatest giants, ever so many feet high, to the smallest dwarf, not bigger than my little finger. And before her stood a number of princes and dukes.

The man went and stood among them, and said, " Wife, are you Emperor now ? "

"Yes," said she. " I'm Emperor."

So he went and looked at her well ; and when he had contemplated her for some time, he said, " Ah, wife, how splendid that is, that you should be Emperor ! "

" Man ! " said she, " what are you standing here for ? I'm Emperor now, but I also wanted to be Pope ; so do you go to the carp."

" Oh, wife," said the man, " What is it you're asking? You can't be Pope. There's only one Pope in Christendom ; the carp can't do that for you."

" My good man," said she, " I will be Pope. Go quickly, for I must be Pope this very day."

"No, wife," answered the man; "I don't like to tell him that—that won't do—that's too strong; the carp can't make you a Pope."

"What nonsense, man!" said she; "if he can make me Emperor, he can make me Pope. Go away at once. I'm Emperor, and you are only my husband; will you go directly?"

Then he was frightened, and went. But he felt quite faint, and trembled and shook, and his knees knocked together. The wind was moaning over the land, the clouds were driving, and the horizon was overcast towards the west; the leaves rustled in the trees, the water rose and hissed as if it had been boiling, and splashed against his shoes; and from afar he saw the ships firing signals of distress, as they tossed and knocked about on the waves. Still the sky was a little blue in the middle, but at the sides it was all lurid and copper-coloured, as if at the approach of a terrible storm. So he went timidly up, and said as he stood trembling:

"Oh, fish in the sea, pray listen to me,
    For my wife won't let be as I'd have it be."

"What does she want?" asked the carp.

"Oh!" said the man, "she wants to be Pope."

"Just go home, she's Pope already," said the carp.

So he went home. And when he came there it was like a great church surrounded by a number of palaces. The people were crowding in; the interior was lit up with a thousand candles, and his wife was dressed all over in gold, and sitting on a much higher throne than the last one, and she had three golden crowns on her head. A number of high dignitaries of the church were standing round her, and on each side of her was a row of lights, of which the greatest was as tall and thick as the biggest tower, and the smallest no larger than a little rushlight; and all the Emperors and Kings were on their knees before her kising her slipper.

"Wife," said the man, as he looked at her, "are you Pope, now?"

"Yes," she said, "I'm Pope."

So he went and had a good look at her, and she shone.

so that it was like looking at the bright sun. When he had looked at her for some time, he said :

" Wife, how capital it is that you're Pope ! " But she was as stiff as a post, and never moved or stirred.

Then he said, " Wife, now be content, now that you're Pope, for now you can't be anything higher."

" I'll think about that," said the wife. And with that they went to bed. But she was not contented—ambition would not let her sleep, and she was always thinking of what she might yet become.

The husband slept soundly and well, for he had run about a good deal the day before ; but the wife could not go to sleep at all, and kept throwing herself from side to side the whole night long, considering what she might yet become, and could think of nothing. In due time the sun began to rise ; when she saw the morning red, she sat up in bed and looked at the light ; and when she saw through the window the sun rising, she thought, " Ha, could not I command the sun and the moon to rise ? "

" Husband," she said, and gave him a dig with her elbow in the ribs, " wake up ; go to the carp and tell him I want to control the sun and moon."

The man was still half asleep ; but he was so frightened that he fell out of bed. He thought that he had misunderstood her, so he rubbed his eyes and cried, " What was it you said, wife ? "

" Husband," she said, " if I can't order the sun and the moon to rise, and have to look on and see them rise, I can't stand it ; I shan't have an hour's quiet, because I can't have them rise when I want."

And she looked at him in such a terrible way that he felt a shudder run right over him.

" Go directly," she cried. " I want to be master of the sun and moon."

" Alas, wife ! " said the man, as he fell on his knees before her ; " the carp can't do that. He can make you Emperor and Pope. Just reflect, I beg of you, and remain Pope."

Then she fell in a passion, her hair fluttered about her head in disorder, she tore her clothes, and she gave him a great kick, and screamed : " I can't bear it any longer ; I can't bear it any longer. Will you be off ! "

So he hurried on his clothes, and ran off like a man demented.

Without, there was a great storm roaring and rushing, so that he could hardly stand on his feet ; houses and trees were torn down, the hills shook, great fragments of rock rolled down into the sea, and the sky was as black as pitch ; it thundered and lightened, and the sea rose in great black billows as high as mountains and church steeples, each wave being capped with a wreath of white foam. Then he cried out, though he could not hear his own words for the tumult :

> " Oh, fish in the sea, pray listen to me,
>   For my wife won't let be as I'd have it be."

" Well, what does she want ? " asked the carp.

" Oh," said he, " my wife wants to be master of the sun and moon."

" Just go home," said the carp, " she's back in the old hovel already."

And there they have remained to this day.

The Six Servants

IN olden times there lived a Queen who was a wicked sorceress and whose daughter was the loveliest girl under the sun. The old woman's only thought was how she could snare men to ruin, and when a suitor appeared, she would say no one except the man who could solve a certain problem should have her daughter. Many were dazzled by the beauty of the girl, and tried to perform the impossible task set them by the old sorceress, but always without success, and each had been obliged to kneel at her feet and have his head cut off.

A certain young Prince then heard of the girl's beauty, and said to his father, " I beg you, let me go and win her."

" Never, never," answered the King. " If you go, you go to certain death."

So the son took to his bed and was an invalid for seven years, and no doctor did him the least good.

When his father saw there was no hope of his getting better he said sorrowfully, " Go if you like and try your luck. I don't know what else to advise."

So the son got up from his couch, perfectly well, and set out in gay spirits.

It happened that as he rode over a common he saw something on the ground in front like a great mound. This, when he came nearer, proved to be a very stout fellow who was lying stretched on the ground.

The fat man, when he saw the horseman, stood up and said : " If you want anyone as a servant, take me."

The Prince asked, " What could I do with such a clumsy attendant ? "

" Oh," said the fat man, " that's nothing to you so long as I behave myself well. If I like I can make myself a thousand times fatter."

" If that's the case," said the Prince, " come with me ; I think you may serve my purpose."

So he went on, followed by the fat man. At a little distance he came to another man lying stretched on the grass with his ear pressed against the ground.

" What are you doing ? " asked the Prince.

" I am listening," answered the man.

" And what are you listening to so attentively ? "

" I am listening to all that is going on in the world. I have such keen hearing that nothing escapes me. I can even hear the grass grow."

" Well, I should like to know," said the Prince, " what you hear going on at the court of the old Queen with the beautiful daughter. Can you tell me ? "

" Yes. I hear the swish of the sword that is being sharpened to cut off a suitor's head."

Then the King's son said, " You will be useful to me, so come along."

So the three pursued their road.

Next a pair of feet was seen in the distance, and parts of the legs could be seen also, but the rest was invisible. After walking a good way they came to the body and the head too.

" Good gracious ! " exclaimed the Prince, " what a long Tom you are ? "

" Yes," was the answer, " but when I stretch my limbs out properly I am three thousand times as long, and taller than the highest mountain on earth. If you'll engage me, I'll serve you well."

" Come along, then," replied the Prince. " You may be useful."

So they all went on together and came to a man sitting by the roadside with his eyes bound up. The Prince asked if he had weak eyes and was unable to bear the light.

" No, indeed," he answered. " I have such marvellously sharp sight that I am obliged to keep the bandage on ; otherwise everything I looked at would dash to bits. If such a gift is of any service to you, take me with you."

" Come along," said the Prince. " You may be useful."

They went on and next came across a man lying in the

sun, shivering and shaking as if he were frozen. Not a limb of him was still.

"What makes you shiver?" asked the Prince. "The sun is so hot."

"Ah," answered the man, "my nature is different from other people's. The warmer the weather the colder I am and the more I shiver; and when the weather is cold I become hot. On ice I cannot breathe for heat, and in the middle of a furnace I am so cold I don't know what to do."

"You are a wonderful fellow certainly," said the Prince. "If you would like to be my servant, come along."

They went on and came to a man with such a long neck that he was standing peering round him over all the mountains.

"What are you looking at so intently?" asked the Prince.

"I have such bright, keen eyes," he replied, "that I can see over woods and fields, mountains and valleys, to the very end of the world."

The Prince then said, "Come with me. It would not do to pass by such a curiosity."

Soon the Prince with his six extraordinary servants arrived in the town where the old Queen lived. Without saying who he was, he told the Queen that if she gave him her lovely daughter he would fulfil any task she might impose on him.

The sorceress was delighted at another fine and gallant youth falling into her snare, and said, "I will make a threefold condition; fulfil it, and you shall be my daughter's lord and husband."

"What is the first part?" asked the Prince.

"You are to bring me a ring that I have dropped into the bottom of the Red Sea."

The Prince went home to his servants and said, "The first thing to be done is not easy. A ring must be fished out of the Red Sea. How is it to be accomplished?"

The man with bright eyes said, "I'll look and see the spot it lies on." He looked and announced that he saw the ring hanging on a sharp stone.

The tall, lanky man said. "I could easily fetch it out if I could see it."

" If that's all," cried the fat man, " I can help." He stooped down and held his mouth open over the water. The waves broke into it as if it had been a cave, and so he drank up the whole sea and left it as dry as a meadow.

Then the long man stooped a little and picked up the ring with his hand.

The Prince in high delight took the ring to the old sorceress.

She was naturally astounded and said, " Yes, that's the right ring. The first part of the condition you have accomplished ; now comes the second. Do you see over there, grazing on the meadow in front of my castle, three hundred fat oxen ? These you are to devour, hair, horns, bones and all. And in the cellars below are three hundred casks of wine. These you must drink every drop of, otherwise I shall have you killed."

" Mayn't I invite a guest to the banquet ? " asked the Prince. " Without company no meal is very appetising."

The old woman laughed evilly.

" You may invite one person," she said, " but only one."

The Prince returned to his servants and said to the fat man, " You are to be my guest to-day and eat yourself full for once."

The fat man then unbelted himself and became a thousand times bigger. He had no trouble in putting away the three hundred oxen, and when he had swallowed the last bone asked if there were not another course. He then drank all the wine out of the casks, not leaving so much as a drop hanging on the tap.

The old woman exclaimed, when she learnt that he had performed the second part of the condition, " So far no one else has done as much as you ! But now comes the third point, and this is the hardest of all and will certainly cost you your head."

Then she said, " This evening I shall bring my daughter to your room and leave her there, and you may sit with your arms round her. But be careful that you keep awake. I shall come again at twelve, and if in the meantime she has vanished you are lost."

The Prince thought, " This part of the condition sounds

easy and pleasant. I shall not be likely to close my eyes."
He nevertheless called his servants and confided in them
what the old creature had said.

"There is no knowing what cunning lies behind the
proposal," he remarked. "One cannot be too careful.
So keep watch and be careful that the maiden doesn't
escape from my chamber."

At nightfall the sorceress brought her daughter and put
her in the Prince's arms ; then the lanky one twisted
himself in a circle round the pair, and the fat man stationed
himself at the door so that no living soul could come in.
There the two sat and the girl did not speak a word, but
the moonlight shone through the window and lit up her
lovely face. The Prince could do nothing but look at her
beauty, full of joy and love, and no fatigue visited his eyes.
This lasted till eleven o'clock, when the old Queen cast a
spell over them and they all fell asleep, and at that moment
the girl was taken away. They slept on till a quarter to
twelve, when the spell lost its power and they awoke.

"Oh, misery and misfortune," cried the Prince. "Now
I am lost indeed."

The faithful servants began to wring their hands, but
the listener with the sharp hearing said, "All be quiet
and let me listen."

He listened for a moment, and then reported : "She is
sitting within a rock three hundred hours' journey from
here and laments her fate. You alone can help her, lanky
one ; two or three strides will take you there."

"Yes," answered the lanky one, "but the sharp-eyed
man must come also to smash down the rocks."

So the lanky man picked up the man with the bandage
over his eyes, and in a second, before you had time to
snap your fingers, they were standing by the enchanted
rock. At once the lanky man removed the bandage from
his companion's sharp eyes, and with one glance the
rock was shivered to atoms. The lanky man then took
the maiden up, carried her back in a moment, went again
for his comrade, and just as twelve struck they were all
in their places as they had been before the spell.

The old sorceress slunk in with a sneering smile, as
much as to say, "Now he must be mine," for she thought

her daughter hundreds of miles away inside the rock. But when she saw the girl in the Prince's arms she was frightened and muttered, "Here's a man who can do greater wonders than I."

There was nothing now to be done but to give her daughter to the Prince. But she managed to whisper in her ear, "Shame on you to obey the behests of vulgar people; not to choose your bridegroom of your own free will."

The maiden's proud soul now rose in revolt and she planned revenge. Next morning she ordered three hundred faggots of wood to be collected and set alight, and said that although the threefold condition had been fulfilled she would not marry the Prince till one of his party had sat in the midst of the burning faggots. She imagined not one of the servants would consent to burn for their master's sake, and that he out of love for her would get into the fire himself, and so she would be rid of him.

The servants said to one another, "We have all done something except the shivering fellow; now it is his turn."

So they sent him into the furnace. It burnt for three days, and when the flames subsided there stood the shivering man among the ashes, shaking like an aspen-leaf, blue with cold.

"Such a frost," he said, "I have never experienced in all my life. If it had gone on much longer I should have been frozen to death."

Now there was no escape; the beautiful girl was obliged to take the strange youth for her husband. But when he was leading her to the church the old Queen said, "I cannot bear this disgrace," and she called out the soldiers and sent them to the church to bring back her daughter.

The listener, however, had pricked up his ears and heard what the old woman was saying privately to her officers. "What shall we do?" he said to the fat man.

The latter was ready with a plan, which was to pour out of his mouth a part of the Red Sea that he had swallowed, and this was enough to drown all the armed knights that came riding up to the church.

When the sorceress knew this she sent out large reinforcements, but these fared no better, for the sharp-eyed man took off his bandage and looked at them, and they fell to bits like broken glass.

Now the ceremony proceeded without interruption, and when it was over the six servants took their leave at the church door.

"Your desires are now all fulfilled," they said to their master. "You have no further need of us; we will therefore travel on and seek our fortune."

Half an hour's walk from the Prince's castle there was a village where a swineherd was tending his pigs.

"Do you know what I really am?" the bridegroom asked his wife. "I am not a Prince at all, but a swineherd like that man over there, who is my father. You and I must go and help him now to feed the pigs."

So he alighted with her at the inn and gave instructions that in the night her royal garments were to be taken away, and the landlady gave her a pair of coarse woollen stockings and an old petticoat to put on.

In the morning when she woke up the Princess thought, "I have deserved all this because I have been so proud and haughty," and she quite believed her husband was a swineherd and she went out with him to feed the pigs.

This lasted eight days, and by the end of that time her feet were torn and sore, and she wondered how she could stand it longer. Then some people came one day and asked if she knew who her husband really was, and she said, "Yes, he is a swineherd, and is just gone to drive a bargain in the town."

They then said, "Come with us and we will take you to him." They led her up to the castle, and in the entrance hall her husband stood waiting to welcome her, attired in royal clothes.

At first she did not recognise him, but he took her in his arms and kissed her and said, "I suffered for you so much and now you have suffered a little for me."

Then the wedding feast was given in good earnest, and I wish you and I had been there.

The Goblin Cobblers

A COBBLER, through no fault of his own, had become so poor that at last he had nothing left to make shoes with except one piece of leather. He cut it out and found it would make just one pair ; then he went to bed and said his prayers, and because he had a good conscience, slept soundly.

In the morning, when he had washed and dressed, he went to his table and prepared to work at his shoes, when, to his astonishment, he found them already made. He could not understand at all how it had happened. He took the shoes in his hand and examined them. They were so carefully made that there was not a stitch in the wrong place—they were, in fact, models of good work-manship.

A few minutes later a customer came in and was so pleased with the shoes that he paid more than the usual price for them, so that the cobbler now had enough money to buy leather for four more pairs.

Early the next morning he found the four pairs finished ; and so it went on, whatever he cut out over night was made up by the morning, till in time his business became so prosperous that he was a well-to-do man.

Now it happened one evening, not long before Christmas, that the cobbler said to his wife before going to bed, " Suppose we sit up to-night in order to see whose are the hands that have helped us so much." The wife agreed and lit a candle ; then they hid in a corner of the room behind some garments that were hung there, and watched. As midnight struck two naked little men came in and sat at the cobbler's table. They at once took hold of the work which had been cut out, and with their tiny fingers began sewing, stitching, and hammering, so that the cobbler, full of admiration, could not take his eyes from them. They did not leave off till they had finished the work, when they put everything in order and hurried away.

The next morning the cobbler's wife said, "The little men have made us rich; we must give them some proof of our gratitude. Running about at night as they do, they must be frozen without any clothes. I tell you what we will do—I will make each a little shirt, waistcoat, and trousers, and knit them a pair of stockings, and you shall make them a pair of shoes."

Her husband approved the plan, and in the evening, when the clothing was ready, they placed their present, instead of the cut-out leather, on the table, and then concealed themselves, to see what the little men would say.

At midnight the little men hopped in and were going to set to work at once, but not finding the leather and only the charming little suits of clothes, they showed signs of the greatest delight. Quick as lightning, they put the things on and sang:

> "So decent and smart are we,
> We no more need cobblers be."

And they jumped and danced about over the chairs and tables. At last they danced out at the door, and from that day they never came again, but the cobbler remained well off, and everything he undertook prospered.

The Brave Little Tailor

ONE fine summer morning a little tailor sat at his table in the window and plied his needle with all his strength. A peasant woman came down the street calling, " Good marmalade. Cheap marmalade ! " That sounded tempting to the tailor's ears, and he put his curly head out of the window and shouted, " Come up here, my dear woman, here is a market for your wares ! "

The woman climbed the stairs with her heavy basket to the tailor and unpacked all her pots at his bidding. He examined one after the other, held them to his nose, then said at last, " Weigh me out four ounces, my good woman, or if it's a quarter of a pound I don't mind."

The woman, who had hoped to find a good customer, gave him the quantity he asked for, but went away grumbling and cross.

" This marmalade," cried the tailor, " I will say grace for, and it shall give me an appetite."

He brought the bread out of the cupboard, cut a round off the loaf, and spread the marmalade on it. " That won't taste bad, I know," he said, " but I'll finish this waistcoat before I take a bite."

So he laid the bread and marmalade beside him and stitched on, making in his satisfaction ever longer stitches. Meanwhile the smell of the marmalade attracted the flies, who sat in great hosts on the wall, and then descended in order to taste the good stuff.

" Who invited *you* ? " said the little tailor, and drove them away. But the flies, who did not understand his language, would not be scattered, and only came again in greater force. Then the little tailor lost his temper, and seized a towel and flicked at the flies till no fewer than seven lay dead, with their legs in the air.

" What a fellow you are ! " he said, admiring his own

bravery; "the whole town shall know of your exploit."
And the little tailor with all speed cut himself out a belt,
hemmed it, and on it inscribed the words, "Seven at one
stroke!" "Not only the town," he ejaculated, "but
the whole world shall know it!" And his heart waggled
with excitement like a little lamb's tail.

The tailor put the belt round his loins with the intention of going out into the world, because the workshop
had become too small for his great bravery. Before
starting, he looked round to see if there was anything worth
taking with him, and saw nothing except an old cheese,
which he stuck in his pocket. In front of the door he
noticed a bird caught in a bush; this went into his pocket
too, to keep the cheese company.

Now he stepped out jauntily, and being so light and
small he felt no fatigue. The road led up a mountain,
and when he had reached the highest peak he found sitting
there a powerful giant, who was calmly looking round him.
The tailor went up to him and said pluckily:

"Good-day, comrade; are you sitting there surveying
the great world further on? I am on my way there. Do
you feel inclined to come with me?"

The giant looked with scorn at the tailor. "You
miserable ragamuffin. Puny wretch!" he exclaimed.

"Oh, indeed, you think so, do you? But look here!"
answered the little tailor. And he unbuttoned his coat
and showed the giant his belt. "Read there what sort
of man I am."

The giant read, "Seven at one stroke"; thought it
was *seven men* the tailor had slain at one stroke, and felt
a little more respect for him. But he determined to
test him first; so he took up a stone and crushed it in
his hand till water came out of it.

"Imitate me and do that," said the giant, "if you really
have any strength."

"Only *that?*" said the tailor; "that is mere child's
play." He put his hand in his pocket, drew forth the
soft cheese, and squeezed it till the moisture ran out.

The giant did not know what to say, but he was still
doubtful about the little man's power, so he took a stone
and threw it so high that it went almost out of sight.

"Now," he said, "do that, you wretched dwarf."

"Well thrown, certainly," remarked the tailor; "but your stone fell to earth again. I will show you one that won't come down any more."

He took the bird from his pocket and threw it into the air. The bird, happy at obtaining its freedom, flew off and did not come back. "There, what do you think of that performance, comrade?" asked the tailor.

"You can throw, I don't deny," answered the giant; "but now I'll just prove if you can carry a decent weight."

He led the little tailor to a mighty oak tree, which had been felled and lay on the ground. "If you are strong enough help me to carry this out of the wood."

"With pleasure," said the little man. "You take the trunk on your shoulder, and I will carry the branches, which is the most difficult part."

The giant took the trunk on his shoulder, and the tailor seated himself on a branch, and as the giant could not look round he was obliged to carry not only the whole tree, but the tailor too.

The latter had a very good time behind, whistled gaily, and sang snatches of "Three tailors rode out of the city," as if tree-carrying were the merest child's play.

The giant, after he had carried the heavy burden some distance, was out of breath, and called that he could not go farther and must let the tree fall.

The tailor jumped off, caught hold of the tree with both arms, as if he had been carrying it all the way, and said to the giant, "To think of a big fellow like you not being able to carry the tree!"

They walked on together until they came to a cherry-tree, when the giant grasped the top, where the ripest fruit grew, pulled it down, put it in the tailor's hands, and told him to eat as many cherries as he could. But the little tailor was far too weak to hold the tree. The giant let go, and the tree, springing back into the air, carried the little tailor with it.

When he had jumped again without hurt to the ground, the giant exclaimed, "Hullo! hadn't you the strength to hold that slender stem?"

"It has nothing to do with strength!" the tailor

answered; " do you suppose, after killing seven with one stroke, I couldn't have done it ? I simply jumped over the tree because there was a huntsman aiming at me from behind the bushes. Jump it yourself if you can.'

The giant made an attempt, but could not clear the tree, and remained suspended in the branches; so again the little tailor had the best of it.

The giant then said, " As you are such a brave little fellow, come to our cave and stay the night there."

The little tailor was quite ready, and followed his host. When they arrived at the cave, other giants were there sitting round the fire, and each held a roasted sheep in his hand, and was eating it as if it were a bun. The little tailor thought, " Things are much more advanced here than in my workshop." Then the giant showed him a bed and told him to lie down and rest. But the bed was too big for the tailor and instead of lying in it he crept into a corner. When midnight came, and the giant thought the little tailor was sound asleep, he took an iron nail, ran it with one blow into the bed, and thought he had made an end of the little grasshopper.

At break of day the giants went out into the wood and had forgotten all about the tailor, when he came tripping towards them as lively and unconcerned as ever. The giants were greatly alarmed, believing he would kill them, and they ran away as fast as they could. The little tailor walked on, still following his sharp little nose.

When he had wandered a long way he came to the courtyard of a royal palace, and by that time he was so tired that he flung himself down on the ground and fell asleep. While he lay there people came to stare at him, and read the inscription on his belt, " Seven at one stroke ! "

" Ah ! " they thought, " this must be some great hero. What is he doing here in times of peace ? " They went and informed the King, and said that if war should break out this man would be useful, and he must not be allowed to go away.

The King fell in with the idea and sent one of the courtiers to offer the tailor, when he should wake, a post in his army. The messenger stood watching the sleeper, and on his stretching his legs and opening his eyes, made the offer.

" That was my object in coming here," answered the little tailor. " I am ready to enter the King's service."

He was therefore received with great honour and given a special house to live in. But the other officers were jealous of the tailor, and wished him a hundred miles away. " What would become of us," they said to each other, " if we got to quarrelling with him, and he with every stroke killed seven of us ? We should have no chance." So they resolved to go in a body to the King and tender their resignations. " We are not fit," they explained, " to hold our own against a man who can take seven lives at a blow."

The King, sorry to lose all his faithful servants for the sake of one man, wished he had never set eyes on him, and longed to get rid of him. But he had not the courage to give him notice, for he feared the tailor might slay him and his people and put himself on the throne. He thought a long time ; then at last hit upon a plan. He sent a message to the little tailor to the effect that, as he was such a great, courageous hero, he wished to make him a proposal, which was as follows :

In a certain wood in his dominions lived two giants, who by murder, rapine and plunder worked great mischief, and nobody dared risk their lives in confronting them. If the tailor would overcome and kill these two giants the King promised he would give him the hand of his only daughter in marriage and half his kingdom. He would also give him a force of a hundred knights to assist in the task of killing the giants.

" Think what a lift for a man like you," thought the tailor to himself ; " a beautiful Princess and half a kingdom are not going begging every day."

So he made answer : " Certainly, I will go and overcome the giants. As for the hundred knights, I shall not want them ; a man who can kill seven at a stroke is more than a match for two."

The little tailor set out, and the hundred knights followed. When they came to the outskirts of the wood, he said to his companions, " Stay here while I settle the giants." He ran on alone into the wood, looking to right and left as he went. In a little while he espied the two giants.

They lay under a tree asleep, nearly snoring off the branches overhead. The little tailor busied himself by filling his pockets with stones and climbed up the tree. Half-way up he slid on to a branch immediately over the sleepers' heads, and then let his stones fall on one of the giants' breasts. For a long time the giant did not move, but at last he roused himself and, shoving his companion, asked, " Why are you hitting me ? "

" You are dreaming," replied the other ; " I didn't hit you."

Again they lay down to sleep. Then the little tailor threw a stone on the second giant.

" What's that ? " he cried.   " Why are you pelting me ? "

" I am not pelting you, answered the first, and growled.

They quarrelled a bit, but as they were both tired they let the matter drop, and their eyes closed once more. The little tailor renewed his game, selected his biggest stone, and flung it on the first giant with all his might.

" This is too annoying," shouted the giant. He sprang up like a madman, and pinned his companion to the tree with such force that the tree shook. The other paid him back in the same coin, and they grew so furious that they tore up trees by the roots and hurled them at each other, till at last they both lay dead on the ground.

At once the little tailor jumped off the tree. " A piece of good fortune," he said, " that they didn't tear up the tree I was sitting on."

He drew his sword and inflicted a wound on the breast of both, then he went to the knights and said : " The work is done ; I have put an end to the two giants, but it was a terrible encounter. In self-defence they tore up trees by the roots, but of course that was of no avail against a man who can strike down seven at a blow."

The knights could not believe him until they rode into the wood, where they found the giants swimming in their own blood, and the uprooted trees lying all round.

The little tailor now demanded of the King his promised reward, but the King repented, and racked his brains again for some way of ridding himself of the little man.

" Before you win my daughter and the half of my kingdom," he said, " you must accomplish yet another heroic deed. You must capture a unicorn that is at large in the wood, doing great harm."

" I am even less afraid of a unicorn than of two giants," boasted the tailor.

He took a halter and an axe and started for the wood, telling the party that was sent with him to wait outside. He had not long to look ; the unicorn came in sight immediately and made straight for the tailor.

He stood still and waited till the animal was quite close, then sprang nimbly behind a tree. The unicorn made a frantic rush at the tree, and gored it with his horn so firmly that he could not get it out again, and was caught.

" Now I've got you, my bird," said the tailor, coming out from behind the tree. He laid the halter round the animal's neck, then hewed its horn out of the tree, and led it home to the King.

But the King would not yet grant the promised reward, and made a third condition. Before his wedding was fixed the tailor must go into the wood again and catch a wild boar that was doing great damage there.

" I will go with pleasure," said the tailor ; " hunting a wild boar is child's play."

When the boar saw the tailor, it ran towards him, foaming at the mouth, with gnashing teeth, ready to knock him over. The nimble hero, however, skipped into a chapel that stood near, and out again in a twinkling through the window. The boar followed, but the tailor flew round outside and shut the door, so that the enraged brute was entrapped, for he was too heavy and not agile enough to jump through the window.

The hero then went to the King and told him that whether he liked it or not he was obliged now to keep his promise and give him his daughter and half his kingdom.

The wedding was celebrated with great magnificence, but with little rejoicing, and the tailor became a King.

Soon afterwards the young Queen heard her husband one night talking in his sleep. " Boy," he called, " just finish off this waistcoat and stitch these trousers for me at once, or I'll hit you over the head with the yard-measure." Then she discovered in what station of life her lord and master had been born, and complained the next morning to her father that she had been allowed to marry a husband who was only a tailor.

The King comforted her by saying, " To-morrow night leave your dressing-room door open ; my servant shall wait outside, and when he is asleep my servants shall creep in and bind him, and put him on board a ship that will bear him to the other end of the world."

The tailor-King's page had heard what the other King said, and disclosed the plot to his master.

" Ah ! " he exclaimed, " I will put a stop to that little affair."

At night he went to bed at the same time as usual and lay down by his wife. She, when she thought he slept, got up, opened the dressing-room door, and lay down again. The little tailor, who was only pretending to be asleep, began to sing out in a shrill voice, " Boy, finish off that waistcoat and stitch those trousers, or I'll hit you with the yard-measure over the ears. I have killed seven at one blow, slain two giants, caught a unicorn and a wild boar ; is it likely I should be afraid of anyone in that dressing-room ? " When the little tailor was heard saying this, everybody was frightened, and the men who were going to bind him scampered off, and not a single soul ever dared make an attempt to touch him again. Thus the brave little tailor remained King to the end of his days.

King Throstle-Beard

A KING had a daughter who was beautiful beyond description, but so haughty and disagreeable that no suitor was good enough for her. She not only rejected one lover after another, but poked fun at them.

Once the King gave a great feast, and invited all the marriageable bachelors to come to it from far and near. They were all ranged in a line according to their rank. First came the kings, then the princes, dukes, counts, and barons, and, last of all, the pages. The King's daughter moved down the line, but to every one she had some objection to make. This one was too fat, " Beer-barrel," she ejaculated scornfully; that one too tall and thin, " Daddy-long legs," was her comment on him. Another was too short—" Short and stout and awkward," she said. The fourth was too pale and " A death's head "; a fifth too red—" A turkey-cock." The sixth was not upright enough—" Like a piece of bent wood behind the stove "; and so on.

But the one she made especially merry over was a King with a crooked chin. " Good gracious ! " she exclaimed, laughing, " the fellow has a chin like a throstle's beak." And from that day the King was given the name of Throstle-beard. The old King, when he saw that his daughter did nothing but make game of people, and that she despised all her suitors, grew very angry, and swore she should marry the first beggar who came to his gates.

A few days later a wandering musician began to sing for alms under the window. The King heard him and ordered the man to be brought in. The musician came in his dirty, ragged clothes, sang before the King and his daughter, and then asked for some small reward.

The King said, " Your song has pleased me so much that I will give you my daughter's hand in marriage."

47

The Princess shuddered, but the King went on, " I
made a vow that I would give her to the first beggar-
man who came this way, and I will hold to my vow."

It was no good to resist. The clergyman was sent for
and the Princess was united to the wandering musician.

After the marriage the King said, " Now you are a
beggar's wife, it is no longer seemly for you to stay in
the castle. You and your husband must go at once."

The beggar led her out by the hand, and she was obliged
to accompany him on foot. They came to a great wood,
and the Princess asked, " To whom belongs this wood, I
wonder ? "

The musician replied :

> " It belongs to the good King Throstle-beard ;
> Hadst thou taken him it would be thine."

And she answered :

> " I, a poor maiden gently reared,
> Ah, would I had taken King Throstle(beard."

Then they came to a meadow and she asked again,
" To whom belongs this pretty green meadow ? "

> " It belongs to the good King Throstle-beard ;
> Hadst thou taken him it would be thine."

And again she sighed :

> " I, a poor maiden gently reared,
> " Ah, would I had taken King Throstle-beard."

Then they came to a big town, and again she asked,
" To whom belongs this beautiful town ? "

> " It belongs to good King Throstle-beard ;
> Hadst thou taken him it would be thine."

To which she replied :

> " I, a poor maiden gently reared,
> How I wish I had taken King Throstle-beard,"

"I am displeased," said the musician, "at your wishing so continually for another husband. Am I not enough?"

At last they reached a very small house, and she exclaimed:

> "The smallest house I did ever see,
> Whose, pray, may this hovel be?"

The musician answered, "It is my house and yours, where we are going to live together."

She was obliged to stoop so as not to bump her forehead as she went in at the low little door.

"Where are the servants?" asked the Princess.

"What servants?" answered the beggar. "You'll have to do everything for yourself. Look sharp, now; light the fire, put the water on to boil, and then cook my supper. I am precious tired."

But the Princess knew nothing about making fires and cooking meals, and the beggar-man was obliged to lend a helping hand, or nothing would have been done. After their frugal supper they went to bed, but early the next morning he made her turn out to do the housework.

For a few days they lived in this fashion, consuming all their provisions, and then the man said, "Look here, wife, this can't go on. We are eating a lot and earning nothing. You shall plait baskets."

He went out, cut some osiers, and brought them home; his wife began to plait, but the rough osiers tore and scratched her delicate hands.

"I see," he said, "that won't do. You shall spin instead; perhaps you will be able to spin better than you can plait."

She sat down and attempted to spin, but the hard threads cut her soft fingers, and the blood poured from them.

"You see," he said, "how it is. You are no good for any work, and I have made a bad bargain in marrying you. Now I must try and start a trade in pots and pans and earthenware articles. You must sit in the market and sell them."

"Oh, dear," thought she; "suppose anyone from my

father's kingdom should come to the market and see me selling pots and pans, how they would jeer at me!"

But there was no help for it; the only alternative was to die of hunger. The first time she did well, for people bought things from the woman because she was pretty, and willingly paid the price she asked—indeed, several gave her the money and made her a present of the pots.

The two lived on her earnings as long as they lasted, and then the man bought another lot of earthenware and crockery. She sat in a corner of the market-place, arranged her wares, and offered them for sale. Then suddenly a drunken soldier, whose horse was running away, rode into her stall, and smashed all the pots to atoms. She began to cry and was in despair as to what she should do. "Oh, dear, what will become of me?" she moaned. "What will my husband say?" And she ran home and told him of her misfortune.

"Tears are not fitting in the eyes of a vendor of earthenware," said her husband. "You are not suited to any proper work. I have been, therefore, to the palace of our King, and asked if you could not be employed there as kitchen-maid. They have promised to give you a trial, and you will get your board for nothing."

So the Princess became a kitchen-maid. She had to drudge for the cook, and do the dirtiest work. She kept in a pocket under her dress a jar with a stopper, in which she took home savings and scraps, and on these she lived.

It happened that the King's eldest son was to give a ball in honour of his coming of age. On the great night the poor young woman went upstairs to look on from behind the doors of the salon. As she saw the lights lit one after the other, and all the beautiful people in beautiful dresses being announced, she almost wept at the dazzling splendour of everything, and thought with sorrow of her own wretched fate, repenting bitterly her haughty and discourteous behaviour, which had plunged her into such poverty. From the costly dishes which were carried to and fro, the delicious smell of which made her mouth water, the waiters now and then threw her a few scraps, and these she put in her jar, with the intention of taking them home.

When the King's eldest son walked into the salon, arrayed in velvet and silk, with jewels and a gold chain round his neck, he saw the poor woman peeping from behind the door, and took hold of her hand and asked her to dance with him. But she refused, trembling, for she recognised King Throstle-beard, the suitor who had wooed her and whom she had held up to ridicule and scorn. But in spite of her struggles, he insisted on drawing her into the hall, when the string that secured the pocket under her dress gave way. Her jar rolled out and the soup and scraps fell all over the floor. The people laughed, and she became the object of general amusement. She wished herself a thousand miles under the earth, she felt so ashamed. She rushed to the door, longing to escape, but on the staircase a man stopped her and brought her back, and when she looked at him, he, too, had the face of King Throstle-beard. In a kind and friendly voice he said to her :

" Don't be afraid. I and the fiddler with whom you lived in the wretched hovel are one and the same person. I disguised myself for love of you ; I, too, was the drunken soldier who rode into your stall and knocked over your pots. These things have happened to break your haughty spirit, and to punish you for your pride."

She wept and sobbed bitterly. " I was very wrong," she said, " and I am not worthy to be your wife."

He, however, comforted her. " The past is over," he said. " Now we will celebrate our wedding feast in good earnest."

At this ladies-in-waiting came and arrayed her in splendid clothes, and her father and his whole court came and wished her joy on her marriage with King Throstle-beard.

Mother Holle

A WIDOW had two daughters, one of whom was pretty and industrious, the other ugly and lazy. She had, however, a much greater affection for the ugly and lazy daughter, because she was her own daughter; the other had to do all the work, and was the Cinderella of the household. The poor girl was obliged to go out on the high-road every day and sit by a well and spin till her fingers bled.

Now it happened once that the spindle became blood-stained, and when she went to the well to wash it, the spindle dropped out of her hands and fell in. Crying, she ran to her stepmother and told of her misfortune. The stepmother scolded her violently, and said she would not forgive her till she had fetched the spindle out of the well again. The girl went back to the well, not knowing what to do. At last, in her fear of more scolding, she plunged into the well. She lost consciousness, and when she came to herself she was lying on a green meadow in the sunshine, surrounded by thousands of lovely flowers. She rose and walked across the meadow till she came to a bake-oven full of bread.

The bread said, " Take me out, take me out, or I shall burn. I've been baking so long."

The girl advanced, and with the bread-shovel took all the loaves out one after the other. Then she went farther, and came to a tree laden with apples, which cried, " Shake me, shake me ; we apples are all too ripe."

So she shook the tree, and the apples rained down by hundreds, till there were no more left on the tree. Then she gathered them in a heap and went on.

At last she came to a small house. An old woman peeped out of the window at her, but she had such big teeth that the girl was frightened and wanted to run away.

The old woman called out, " Why are you frightened, dear ? Stay with me, and if you will do my house-work properly you shall have a nice home here. You must be careful to make my bed well and shake the mattress till the feathers fly about, and then it will snow in the world. I am Mother Holle."

Because the old woman spoke so kindly, the girl took heart, and consented to enter her service. She performed all her duties to the old woman's satisfaction, and shook up the mattress till the feathers flew about like snow-flakes ; so she had a comfortable home, and had meat, either boiled or roasted, every day for dinner.

After a time, she grew sad, and did not know at first what was the matter, but at last she was certain it was home-sickness ; although it was a thousand times pleasanter at Mother Holle's than at home, yet she had a longing to go. At last she said, " I have a great yearning for home, and though I like everything down here very much, I cannot stay, but must go up to my own people."

To which Mother Holle replied : " I am pleased to hear you say you wish to go home, and as you have served me well and faithfully I will take you up myself."

She took her by the hand and led her to a great gate-way. The gate opened, and as the girl was standing just under it, a shower of gold fell over her, and all the gold hung on her clothes, so that she was covered from head to foot.

" You shall have all this because you have been so industrious," said Mother Holle, and gave her, besides, the spindle which she had let fall into the well.

Suddenly the gate was shut with a bang, and the girl was up above in the world again, not far from her mother's house. When she came into the yard the cock sat on the pump and cried :

" Cock-a-doodle-do.
Our golden girl has come home again."

Then the girl went in to her mother, and because she was covered with gold she and her sister received her kindly. The girl told them all her adventures, and, hearing how she had come into such riches, the mother planned that her ugly, lazy daughter should get her share too. She sent her to spin by the well, and, to make her spindle bloodstained, she pricked her finger and put her hand into a hedge of thorns. Then she threw the spindle down the well and jumped in after it.

Like the other, she came to the beautiful meadow and followed the same path. But when she reached the bake-oven and the bread shouted, "Take me out, take me out, or I shall burn," the lazy girl answered, "I don't want to dirty myself, thank you," and continued her walk.

Soon she came to the apple-tree, which cried as before, "Shake me, shake me; we apples are all too ripe."

She answered, "I dare say; but an apple might fall on my head," and went on.

When she came to Mother Holle's little house she was not afraid, because she had been warned that the Dame had big teeth. The first day the ugly girl tried hard to be industrious and to obey the wishes of Mother Holle, because she thought of all the gold that was to be her reward; on the second day, however, she began to be idle; on the third she was worse, as she almost refused to get up early in the morning, and she forgot to make Mother Holle's bed properly and to shake the mattress till the down flew about. Mother Holle by that time was tired of her, and gave her notice. The lazy girl was quite content, and thought, "Now it's time for the gold rain!"

Mother Holle led her to the gateway, but as she stood under it, instead of gold, a great kettle of pitch was poured over her. "That is in reward for your services," said Mother Holle, and shut the gate.

So the lazy girl went home covered with pitch, and the cock on the pump, when he saw her, exclaimed:

> "Cock-a-doodle-do.
> Our dirty girl has come home again."

The pitch wouldn't wash off, and it stuck to her till the end of her days.

The Bottled Spirit

THERE was once a poor wood-cutter who worked from early morning till late at night. When at last he had scraped together a little money he said to his boy, " You are my only child, so I will give you the money I have earned with the sweat of my brow to spend on your education. Learn something useful, then you will be able to support me in my old age when my limbs are too stiff for me to do anything but sit by the fireside."

The boy went to a school and studied diligently. His teachers praised him for his industry and he stayed there some time. Then he went to college, but before he was perfect in everything he was obliged to leave, for his father's savings had run out. He came home, and his father said sorrowfully, " I can do no more for you, and now can earn nothing beyond what is necessary for our daily bread."

" Dear father," answered the son, " don't worry about it. If God so wills, it must be for the best." And when the old man started to cut down trees the next day he offered to go with him.

" Yes, my son," said his father, " come ; but it will be hard for you, as you are not used to such toil and labour. Besides, I have only one axe and no money to buy another."

" Never mind," said the son, " we will borrow an axe of our neighbour, who will, I am sure, let me keep it till I earn a new one."

So the father borrowed an axe from his neighbour, and at break of day they went together into the forest. The son helped his father and was in gay spirits.

When the sun was high in the heavens the old man said, " We will rest now and have our lunch. This is the best time."

The son took his portion of bread and then said, " You

rest, father, but I am not tired. I will take a little stroll and look for birds' nests."

" You ninny," exclaimed his father, " if you run about now you'll be too worn out to raise an arm. Better sit by me and rest."

But the son strolled on, ate his bread, and was happy and contented as he looked up in the green branches above him for birds' nests. He walked up and down till he saw a fine oak of gigantic circumference which was hundreds of years old. He stood still and thought, " Many a bird must have built a nest there."

Then he fancied he heard a voice. He listened hard and it certainly was a muffled voice saying, " Let me out ! let me out ! " He looked round, but could discover nothing, and it seemed as if the voice came from the ground. So he called, " Where are you ? "

The voice answered, " I am here, under the oak roots. Let me out ! Let me out ! "

The student began to dig among the roots, and at last came to a small hollow in which he found a glass bottle. He raised it in the air and held it against the light. There was a thing inside like a frog, jumping frantically up and down. " Let me out ! Let me out ! " it cried again, and the youth, meaning no harm, drew out the cork. Immediately a spirit came out of the bottle, grew and grew till a terrible fellow, half as tall as the tree, stood before the student.

" Do you know," he said in gruff and awful tones, "what will be your reward for letting me out ? "

" No," answered the student fearlessly. " How should I know ? "

" I must break your neck for it," answered the spirit.

" A pity you didn't say so a little sooner, and I would have let you stay where you were. As for my head, you will leave it alone, as other people must be consulted before you touch it."

" People or no people, you must have the reward you richly deserve. Do you think I was imprisoned there for nothing ? No, it was my punishment. I am the mighty Merkurius ; whoever frees me is bound to have his neck broken."

"All right," said the student coolly, "but even that cannot be done in a hurry. First, I must have proof that it was really you, great hulking fellow, who sat in that small bottle. If you can get in again I shall be convinced, and you can then do what you like with me."

The spirit answered loftily, "A very simple trick," and he shrank and shrank till he was thin and small enough to creep through the opening of the bottle. Scarcely was he inside before the student deftly screwed the cork in and flung the bottle into its old place under the roots of the oak. The spirit was checkmated.

The student now intended to join his father again. The spirit, however, squealed piteously. "Oh, let me out! Let me out!" The student said, No, he would do nothing of the sort. But the spirit made him listen to argument. He promised not to break his neck, but to give him wealth that would last his life long.

"I dare say," said the young man. "You would only deceive me in the same way again."

"You are wrecking your own chances of happiness by refusing," declared the spirit. "I swear not to touch a hair of your head."

The student then thought, "I'll risk it. Perhaps he will keep his word." So he took the cork out, and the spirit grew taller and taller, as before.

"Now you shall have your reward," said the giant; and he handed the student a case of plaster, saying, "If you touch a wound with one end, it will heal; and if you strike steel or iron with the other end, it will change either into silver."

"Let me try it first," said the student, and went to a tree, from which he hewed off a bit of bark with his axe, then touched the place with the plaster, and the bare place became covered with bark again. "It is genuine," he said to the giant. "Now we may separate."

The spirit thanked him for rescuing him, and the student thanked the spirit for his present, and they went their several ways.

When the student came back his father grumbled, and asked what he meant by neglecting his work so long. "I told you you would never make anything of it," he said.

"Don't disturb yourself, father; I'll soon make up the time I've wasted."

"Make up!" repeated the father wrathfully; "how, I should like to know?"

"Look out, father; I'll have that tree down with one blow!" He took his plaster and rubbed the axe with it, then struck; but because the iron had turned into silver the blade of the axe bent. "I say, father, look what a bad axe you borrowed; it is all crooked."

The father looked aghast and said, "A pretty mess you've made of it! Now you will have to pay for the axe, and where the money is to come from I don't know. You have certainly been a lot of help."

"Don't be vexed," said the son, "I shall be able to pay for the axe."

"Oh, you blockhead!" cried the father, "how will you pay? You have no money. Your brains may be good, but you understand nothing about wood-cutting."

After a while the student remarked, "Father, I can't work any more, let us have a half-holiday."

"Eh, what?" answered his father. "Do you think I can afford to twiddle my thumbs? I am bound to work; but you may as well go home, for you are no good."

"But, father, this is the first time I've been in the forest. I can't find my way alone. Come with me, please," he said, and, the father's anger having cooled a little, he consented to go home.

Then he said to his son, "Go and sell the damaged axe and see what you can get for it; the rest I must earn in order to make the loss good to my neighbour."

The son took the axe and carried it to a goldsmith's in the town, who tried it, laid it on the scales, and said, "It is worth four hundred thalers, and I haven't so much in cash to give you."

The student said, "Well, give me as much as you have; the rest I'll lend to you."

So the goldsmith gave him three hundred thalers and remained a hundred in his debt.

Then the student went home and said, "Father, I have the money. Go and ask what the neighbour will take for his axe."

"I know without asking," answered the old man; "one thaler and six groschens."

"Well, then, give him two thalers and twelve groschens; that will be double," the son said. "You see I have a lot of money," and he gave his father one hundred thalers, saying he should now never want for anything, but live in comfort always.

"Good gracious!" exclaimed the old man, "where did this wealth come from?"

Then the son told how things had happened. With the remainder of the money he went back to college; and in time, because his plaster could heal all wounds, he became the most famous physician in the world.

The Spindle, The Shuttle and The Needle

A YOUNG girl had lost her parents when she was very young. She had a godmother, who lived all alone in a little cottage at the end of the village, and lived on what she earned by her needle, her spindle, and her shuttle. This good woman had taken the orphan home, and had taught her to work, and brought her up in piety and the fear of God.

When the young girl was fifteen years old her godmother fell sick. She called the child to her bedside and said, "Dear child, I feel that my end is near. I leave you my cottage; it will protect you against wind and rain. I also give you my spindle, my shuttle, and my needle, which will enable you to earn your living."

Then placing her hand upon the girl's head she blessed her, and said, "Keep your heart pure and honest, and happiness will come to you." Then her eyes closed; the poor girl went weeping beside her godmother's coffin to the graveside.

After this she lived all alone, working bravely at weaving, spinning, and sewing; and the blessing of the good old woman kept her from harm. One would have thought that her stock of flax would never run out, and as soon as she had woven a piece of stuff, or made a shirt, a purchaser was sure to come and pay well for it; so that not only was she free from want, but had even something to give to the poor.

About this time the King's son came roaming through the country in search of a wife. He could not choose a poor one, and he did not like a rich one. So he said he would choose the girl who was at the same time the poorest and the richest. On coming to the village where our young girl lived, he asked, according to his wont, to be shown the poorest and the richest girl in the place. The richest was quickly found ; as for the poorest, they told him it must be the young girl who lived in the lonely cottage at the end of the hamlet.

When the Prince passed by the rich girl was sitting dressed in her best in front of her door ; she rose and went towards him with a profound curtsey. But he looked at her, and without a word passed on. He then came to the cottage of the poor girl ; she was not at the door, but shut up in her room. He stopped and looked through the window into the room, which a ray of the sun lighted up. She was sitting at her spinning-wheel, working industriously. On her part she secretly observed the Prince looking at her ; but she blushed scarlet, and continued spinning with her eyes cast down ; only I won't warrant that her thread was quite even. She went on spinning until the Prince was gone. So soon as she had lost sight of him, she ran to open the window, saying, "It's so hot here!" and she followed him with her eyes as long as she could perceive the plume on his hat.

At last she sat down again and resumed her spinning. But a rhyme she had often heard her old godmother sing came into her mind, and she sang :

> "Run without stopping, spindle dear,
> See that thou bring my true love here!"

And what happened ? The spindle sprang suddenly from her hands and rushed out at the door. She followed it with her eyes, quite stupefied with wonder. It ran and danced across the fields, leaving a thread of gold behind it. In a little while it had gone too far for her to see. Having no spindle, she took her shuttle, and began to weave.

The spindle ran on and on, and by the time its thread was all unwound it had overtaken the Prince. "What do I see ?" he cried. "This spindle wants to conduct me somewhere." Turning his horse, he galloped back.

guided by the golden thread. The young girl continued working, singing the while :

> " Run out to meet him, shuttle dear ;
> See thou guide my bridegroom here."

Then the shuttle sprang from her hands and hopped out at the door. But, arrived on the threshold, it began to weave the most splendid carpet ever seen. On each side were garlands of roses and lilies, and in the centre green vines grew out of a golden ground. Hares and rabbits were represented jumping in the leaves, and stags and squirrels looked out from among them. On the branches were perched birds of a thousand hues, who only wanted voice to make them perfect. The shuttle went on running and the carpet-weaving advanced marvellously.

As she had lost her shuttle, the young girl took her needle, and began singing :

> " He's coming, he's coming, my needle dear ;
> See thou that all things are ready here."

The needle jumped from her fingers and began running round the room as quick as lightning. It was as if little invisible spirits had taken up the matter ; the tables and benches covered themselves with green tapestry, the chairs were dressed in velvet, and silken hangings appeared on the walls.

Scarcely had the needle pierced its last stitch when the girl saw the white plume of the Prince's hat pass the window. He had been brought back by the golden thread. He entered the room, stepping over the carpet, and there he saw the young girl still dressed in her poor clothes, but shining among all this sudden splendour like a wild rose on a bush.

" Thou art at once the poorest and the richest," he cried. " Come, thou shalt be my wife."

She held out her hand to him without replying. He gave her a kiss, lifted her on his horse, and carried her off to the court, where their wedding was celebrated with great rejoicings.

As for the spindle, the shuttle, and the needle, they were carefully preserved in the royal treasury.

The Magic Herbs

ONCE upon a time there was a young hunter who went into the wood in search of game. He was of a bright and cheerful disposition, and as he walked along he whistled on a leaf. An ugly old hag appeared and said to him, "Good day, dear hunter; you seem merry and content, but I am hungry and thirsty, so give me a trifle."

The good-natured fellow's pity was excited, and he put his hand in his pocket and gave her a bit of his fortune. Then he wished to walk on, but the old hag held him back and said, "Listen, dear hunter. As you have such a kind heart I will give you a present. Go your way, and after a while you will come to a tree on which sit nine birds with a mantle in their claws. Take aim with your fowling-piece and shoot into the middle of them; they will let the mantle fall, but one of the birds will be hit too, and fall dead on the ground. Take the mantle with you, for it is a wishing-mantle; you have only to throw it over your shoulders and you will find yourself at once in any place you may wish to go to. Take the heart out of the dead bird's breast, and swallow it whole, and you will find every morning when you get up a gold coin under your pillow."

The hunter thanked the wise woman and thought, "She promises me pleasant things. I wonder if they'll come to pass." But he had not gone a hundred steps when he heard a great twittering and calling among the branches, and on looking up saw a number of birds tearing with their claws and beaks at a cloth which they dragged about. They were fighting and disputing as to which of them should have it.

"Really, this is wonderful!" exclaimed the man; "everything is happening as the old crone said it would," and he took aim and fired so that the feathers of the birds thickened the air. The covey took flight, but one bird fell wounded to the earth, and the mantle, too, dropped at his feet. Then the hunter obeyed the old woman's instructions, ripped up the bird, took out its heart, swallowed it whole, and carried the mantle home.

The next morning when he woke he remembered the old woman's prediction, lifted his pillow, and saw the flash of a gold coin.

The next morning he found another, and so it went on till he had a great pile of gold. Then at last he asked himself, "What is the good of all this wealth if I stay at home. I will use it and see the world."

So he bade farewell to his parents, hung up his hunter's wallet and gun, and set off. It happened one day that he came through a dense forest, at the other end of which, lying in the valley, was a very grand castle. In one of its windows an old woman and a beautiful girl stood looking out.

The old woman was a witch, and said to the girl, " There comes a man who has a wonderful treasure in his inside ; we must relieve him of it, daughter dear. It will agree with us better than with him. It is a bird's heart, and every morning he finds a gold coin under his pillow."

She then told the girl her design of robbing him, and the part she was to play in the plot, and with flashing eyes threatened her that if she did not do as she was told it would be the worse for her.

When the hunter drew near he caught sight of the girl at the window, and said to himself, " I have walked a long way, and will ask to be put up in this nice castle. I have money enough to pay for luxurious quarters." But it was the pretty girl in the window that attracted him.

He entered the house, and was warmly welcomed and entertained.

Then the old woman said, " Now we must get hold of that bird's heart ; he will never miss it."

She prepared a hot drink, and when it had boiled poured it into a goblet, which she told the girl to give to the hunter.

" Here, my dearest," she said, " drink my health."

He took the goblet and drained it. When he had reached the dregs the bird's heart came out of his body. The girl picked it up on the sly and swallowed it herself.

From this time forward he found no gold coins under his pillow, but from under the girl's pillow the old witch reaped a rich harvest. The young man, however, was so much in love, that he took no heed of anything but the pretty girl.

Then the old woman said, " We have got the bird's heart ; now we must have the wishing mantle."

The girl answered, " No, let him keep it as he has lost his wealth."

The old woman flew into a passion, and said, " A mantle such as that is a valuable possession. I will and must have it." So she gave the girl blows, and said if she did not obey her she would rue it.

The girl thereupon did the old woman's bidding. She placed herself in the window and gazed at the distant view as if she were miserable.

" Why do you stand there looking so sad ? " asked the hunter.

" Ah, my dear," she gave answer, " over there lie the granite-mountains, where the costliest jewels and precious stones come from. I cherish so great a longing for them that it makes me sad to think how impossible it is to get them. Only the birds that fly can go there. Men never."

" If that is the cause of your sadness," the hunter said, " I can relieve your mind." Thereupon he caught her under his mantle, wished himself at the granite-mountains, and the next instant they were both sitting there. The costliest gems glittered all round them, and they gathered up some of the most precious. But the witch, with her magic, had made the hunter's eyes heavy and weary. He suggested to his companion that they should sit down and rest a little.

" I am so tired," he said, " I am ready to drop." And he laid his head in the girl's lap and fell asleep. When he was in a sound slumber she unfastened the mantle from his shoulders, put it over her own, and, shovelling up her diamonds, rubies, and pearls, wished herself at home.

When the hunter awoke, he saw the trick his lady-love

had paid him, and that he was alone and deserted on the strange mountains.

The mountain he was on belonged to some monstrous giants who lived there, and he had not been long awake before he saw them striding towards him. He lay down again and shammed being in a deep sleep.

The first giant stumbled on him with his foot, and exclaimed, "Here's a miserable earth-worm lying inside out!"

"Trample on it," said the second.

But the third said, "It's not worth the trouble. Let him be, he can't stay where he is; if he climbs higher to the top of the mountain the clouds will carry him away."

They went on, and the hunter marked what they had said. When they were out of sight he stood up and climbed to the top. He sat there a few minutes and then a cloud floated near: he caught hold of it, and after being wafted about in the sky was dropped into a garden of herbs.

The hunter looked round and said, "I haven't had much to eat lately, and I am hungry; but here is no sign of apples and pears, or fruit of any sort. Nothing but vegetables and herbs."

At last necessity drove him to appease his hunger with a salad. "Though not very nourishing," he reflected, "it will at least refresh me." So he chose a fine lettuce, ate some, and at once experienced an extraordinary sensation. He felt himself changing utterly. He developed four legs, a thick head, and two long ears. To his horror, he saw that he was now an ass. Still feeling hungry, however, he grazed on another vegetable, and discovered that he was changing again back into his human shape. After that, he lay down and slept off his weariness.

The next morning he took a specimen of both salads. "These," he said to himself, "shall help me to recover my property and punish the unfaithful." So with the bundle of salad in his pocket he went to search for the castle in which his lady-love lived. He found it after two days' wandering. He stained his face brown so that his own mother would not have recognised him, and went up to the castle asking to be taken in. "I am so exhausted," he said, "I cannot go another step."

The witch asked, "What is your business, my good fellow? Who are you?"

"I am one of the King's scouts," he answered, "and I have been sent out to find the most costly salad under the sun. I am thankful to say I have been successful, and have it with me."

At the mention of a choice salad the old witch's mouth watered, and she said, "My dear fellow-countryman, let me taste this wonderful salad."

"Why not?" he said. "I have brought away two bunches, and can easily give you one," and he handed her the dangerous kind.

The witch suspected nothing, and took it into the kitchen to prepare it herself. When it was ready she could not wait till it was on the table, but took a leaf or two and put them in her mouth. Directly she had swallowed it she lost her human form, and ran away across the yard an ass.

Then the servant girl came into the kitchen, and, seeing the salad was ready, took it to carry upstairs, but, from old habit, tasted it on the way, became an ass likewise, and ran after the other into the yard.

Meanwhile the hunter sat waiting with the pretty girl for the salad, but as no one brought it, she said, "I wonder where the salad is."

The hunter thought, "The herb is beginning to act by this time"; then said aloud, "I will go down to the kitchen and inquire for it."

When he got there he saw the two asses rambling about in the yard, and the salad on the floor.

He picked up the remaining leaves, laid them on the dish, and took them up to the girl.

She ate some of it, and, like the others, was at once deprived of her human form, and ran into the yard an ass.

Afterwards the hunter washed his face, so that the transformed ones should recognise him, and, going into the yard, said, "Now you shall pay the penalty of your falseness." So he bound them together with a rope and drove them along till they came to a mill. He tapped on the window-pane, and the miller put out his head and asked what was his business.

" I have three stubborn animals," he answered, " that I can't keep any longer. If you take them off my hands and give them board and lodging I will pay you well."

" All right," said the miller, " but what shall I do with them ? "

Then the hunter told him to give the eldest ass (the witch) three beatings a day and only one meal ; the second ass (the servant girl), one beating and three meals, and the youngest (his former sweetheart) no beating and three meals, for he could not harden his heart to allow the girl to be beaten. After this he returned to the castle and found there all he wanted.

In a few days the miller came and informed him that the old ass who had been given three beatings and only one meal a day, was dead. " The two others," he went on, " are still alive and get three meals, but they are so depressed and sad, I don't think they can last much longer."

The hunter, touched at this, allowed his anger to abate, and told the miller to drive them back to him. When they came he gave them the other bunch of salad to eat, so that they should become human beings again.

Then the pretty girl fell at his feet, and said, " Alas, my love, my mother forced me to do wrong. Pardon me, for I did it against my will. I love you dearly. Your wishing-mantle hangs in a cupboard over there."

This quite pacified him, and he said, " Keep them both, for it is all the same thing. I intend to make you my wife."

So they married, and lived happily together till they died.

Rumpelstiltskin

ONCE upon a time there was a miller who had a very beautiful daughter. She was not only beautiful but shrewd and clever; and her father was never tired of boasting about the wonderful things she could do.

One day, having to go to the palace on business, he told the King that his daughter could spin gold out of straw.

Now the King was very fond of money; and when he heard the miller's boast, he at once ordered the girl to be brought before him. Then he led her to a room where there was a great quantity of straw, gave her a spinning-wheel, and said, "All this straw must be spun into gold before morning; if it is not you will surely be put to death."

It was in vain that the poor maiden declared that she could do no such thing : the door was locked and she was left alone in the room.

She sat down in one corner and began to weep over her hard fate, when suddenly the door opened, and a funny little man hobbled in, and said, "Good morrow, my lass, what are you crying for ? "

"Alas," said she, "I must spin all this straw into gold, and I don't even know how to begin."

"What will you give me," asked the little man, "to spin it for you ? "

"My beautiful necklace," replied the maiden.

The dwarf took her at her word, and sat himself down to the wheel ; round and round it went merrily, and presently the work was done and all the gold spun.

When the King came and saw this, he was greatly surprised and pleased ; but his heart grew still more greedy, and he shut up the poor miller's daughter in another room with a fresh task. She knew not what to do, and sat down once more to weep ; but the little man presently opened the door, and asked, " What will you give me to do your task ? "

"This diamond ring," replied she.

So her little friend took the ring, and worked away at the wheel till by morning all was finished again.

The King was greatly delighted to see all this glittering treasure ; but still he was not satisfied, and took the miller's daughter into a yet larger room, and said, " If all this is spun to-night you shall be my Queen."

As soon as she was alone the dwarf came in, and asked : " What will you give me to spin the gold for you this third time ? "

" I have nothing left to give," said she.

" Then promise me," said the little man, " your first little child when you are Queen."

" That may never be," thought the miller's daughter ; and as she knew no other way to get her task done, she promised what he asked, and he spun once more the whole heap of gold.

The King came in the morning, and finding all he wanted, married her.

At the birth of her first little child the Queen rejoiced greatly, quite forgetting the little man and her promise. But one day he came into her room and reminded her of it. Then she grieved sorely at her misfortune, and offered him all the treasures of the kingdom in exchange ; but in vain, till at last her tears softened him, and he said, " I will give you three days' grace, and if during that time you tell me my name, you shall keep your child."

Now the Queen dispatched messengers all over the land to inquire for new names.

The next day the little man came, and she began with Timothy, Benjamin, Jeremiah, and all the names she could remember ; but to all of them he said, " That's not my name."

The second day she began with all the comical names she could hear of, Bandy-legs, Hunch-back, Crook-shanks, and so on, but the little old gentleman still said to every one of them, " That's not my name."

The third day came back one of the messengers, and

said, " As I was climbing a high hill among the trees of the forest, I saw a little hut, and before the hut burnt a fire, and round about the fire danced a funny little man upon one leg, and sang :

> " To-day I'll brew, to-morrow bake;
> Merrily I'll dance and sing,
> To-morrow will a baby bring:
> The lady cannot stop my game,
> Rumpelstiltskin is my name ! "

When the Queen heard this, she jumped for joy, and as soon as her little visitor came, and asked, " Now, lady, what is my name ? " " Is it John ? " asked she. " No ! " " Is it Tom ? " " No ! "

" Can your name be Rumpelstiltskin ? "

" Some witch told you that ! Some witch told you that ! " cried the little man, and dashed his right foot in a rage so deep into the floor that he was forced to lay hold of it with both hands to pull it out. Then he made the best of his way off, while everybody laughed at him for having had all his trouble for nothing. And the Queen never saw him again.

The Blue Light

THERE was once a soldier who had served his King faithfully for many years. But when peace was proclaimed and the war was over, the King said to the soldier, who had been wounded several times, " Now you can go home ; I require your services no longer. I cannot give you further pay, for I only pay those who earn money."

The poor soldier did not know how he should live. He tramped homewards, and on his way found himself in a great forest. When darkness fell, he saw a light which came from a cottage in which an old witch lived. " Give me a bed and something to eat and drink," he said to her, " otherwise I shall perish."

" Ho, ho," she answered, " who would care to feed a deserter for nothing ? However, I will have compassion on you and take you in, if you will do as I desire."

" What do you desire me to do ? " asked the soldier.

" To dig up my garden to-morrow."

The soldier consented, and worked the next day with all his strength. However, he could not get it done by the evening.

" I see," said the witch, " that you can't do any more to-night, so I will keep you another night, and in return you must chop a clump of wood for me into little pieces."

The soldier took the whole day over it, and in the evening the witch proposed that he should stay another night.

" To-morrow I have only a very light task for you. Behind my house is an old dried-up well into which I have dropped my light, a blue one, which is never extinguished. You shall fetch it for me."

The next day the old crone led him to the well, and lowered him in a basket. He found the blue light, and made a sign to her to draw him up again. She drew him up, but when he reached the edge of the well she held out her hand to seize the blue light. But he, seeing her evil design, said, " No, I shall not give you the light till I am standing with both feet on the ground." Then the witch lost her temper, let him drop into the well again, and went away.

The poor soldier fell, without hurting himself, to the bottom. The blue light still burned, but what help was that? He saw death staring him in the face. For a while he sat lost in sad reflection. Then he chanced to put his hand in his pocket and find his pipe, which was half filled with tobacco. "This shall be my last enjoyment," he said; drew it out, lit it with the blue light, and began to smoke. As the smoke rose and floated on the air, a little black man suddenly appeared and said:

"Sir, what are your orders?"

"Why should I order you about?" asked the soldier, astonished.

"I must do all," said the little man, "that you desire."

"Very well," said the soldier, "help me out of the well."

The little man took his hand and led him through an underground passage, not forgetting to take the blue light too. He showed him on the way the treasure the witch had collected and hidden here, and the soldier helped himself to as much gold as he could carry.

When he was above ground he said to the little man, "Go, please, bind the witch hand and foot, and take her before the judge."

In a few minutes she flashed by on the back of a wild tom cat, screaming horribly, and the mannikin said, "It is all over; by this time she hangs on the gallows."

Then the little man said, "Sir, I await further orders."

The soldier replied, "Just now I have nothing more for you to do; you can go home, only, if I call you, be ready."

"It is not necessary to call," explained the little man, "you have only got to light your pipe with the blue light and I shall be beside you at once." And he instantly vanished.

The soldier went back to the town. He went to the best inn, bought fine clothes, and ordered a room to be splendidly fitted up for him. When it was ready, he summoned the black mannikin and said, "I served the King faithfully, but he sent me away to starve, and now I wish to be revenged on him."

"What am I to do?" asked the little fellow.

"Go in the night to the palace, and bring me the King's daughter to be my maid-servant."

The little man said, " An easy thing for me to do, but a dangerous undertaking for you."

On the stroke of midnight the door sprang open, and the little man brought in the King's daughter.

" Ah, there you are ! " exclaimed the soldier. " Fetch the broom at once and sweep out the room."

When she had finished sweeping, he called her to his arm-chair, stuck out his legs, and bade her take off his boots. He then threw them in her face, and told her to clean and polish them. She did everything without showing a sign of resistance, silently, and with half-closed eyes. At cock-crow the little black man carried her back to the palace and laid her in her bed.

The next morning she went to her father and told him she had had a wonderful dream. " I was carried as quickly as a flash of lightning through the streets and brought into a soldier's room. I was obliged to serve him like a common servant, sweep the room, and brush his boots. Although it was only a dream, I am as tired as if I had really done it."

" Perhaps it was more than a dream," said the King. " Take my advice and fill your pockets full of peas ; then make a tiny hole in the pocket, and if you are fetched again the peas will fall out in the street and show the way."

While the King was speaking the little black man stood by invisible and heard all. At night, when he again carried the sleeping Princess through the streets, some of the peas, it is true, fell on to the pavement, but they had no effect, for the cunning little man had beforehand strewn *all* the streets with peas. The Princess had again to drudge till cock-crow like a common servant.

The next day the King sent out men, but on a fool's errand, for in every street the poor children were picking up peas and saying, " Last night it must have rained peas."

" We must think of another plan," said the King. " Keep on your shoes when you go to bed, and leave one behind at the place you are carried to, and I will have it found."

The black mannikin heard, and when he was requested to bring the Princess to the soldier that night, he said, " I am fairly baffled this time ; if the shoe is found in your oom things may fare badly with you."

"Do as I tell you," answered the soldier.

So for a third night the Princess came and worked like a servant. But before she was carried away she hid one of her shoes under the bed.

The following morning the King had the whole town searched for his daughter's shoe; it was found in the soldier's apartment. The soldier himself, who, acting on the entreaties of the little black man, had hurried out at the town gates, was soon overtaken and cast into prison. In the flight he had forgotten his most priceless property, the blue light and the witch's gold. He only had a few small coins on him. Loaded with chains, he was standing at his prison window when he saw one of his old comrades go by. He tapped on the window-pane, and as the man drew near, said to him, "If you will go to my inn and fetch a small bundle I have left there I will give you something for your trouble." The comrade ran quickly and brought him the bundle. As soon as the soldier was alone, he kindled his pipe with the blue light, and his little black friend stood beside him.

"Don't be afraid," he said, "go with them calmly wheresoever they take you, but don't forget the blue light."

The next day the soldier was tried by the judges, and though he had done nothing wrong, he was condemned to death. When he was brought to the gallows he besought the King to grant him a last favour.

"What sort of favour?" asked the King.

"That I may smoke a pipe on the way."

"You may smoke three pipes; but remember they won't save your life," retorted the King.

The soldier drew out his pipe, lit it with the blue light, and before a ring of smoke had floated on the air, the little man, with a cudgel in his hand, stood before him saying, "What orders, my master?"

"Strike the false judges to the ground, and do not spare the monarch who has treated me so shamefully," was the command.

The small man lashed about with fury, and felled every-one round him to the earth. The King grovelled on the ground, and, in order to save his life, promised the soldier his kingdom and his daughter.

One-Eye, Two-Eyes, and Three-Eyes

THERE was a woman who had three daughters, of whom the eldest was called One-eye, because she had only one eye, in the middle of her forehead ; the next one Two-eyes, because she had two eyes like other people ; and the youngest Three-eyes, because she had three eyes, and the third was likewise in her case in the middle of her forehead. But because Two-eyes did not look any different from other human beings, her mother and sisters could not bear her. They said to her, " You, with your two eyes, are no better than the common folk ; you do not belong to us." They pushed her about and threw her old clothes, and gave her nothing to eat but the scraps left over, and made her suffer in every way they could.

It happened that Two-eyes had to go out into the field to tend the goat, but was very hungry, because her sisters had given her so little to eat. So she sat down on a ridge and began to weep, and wept so much that two little streams flowed from her eyes. And once when she looked up in her distress, a woman stood by her who asked, " Two-eyes, why do you weep ? "

Two-eyes answered, " Why should I not cry ? Just because I have two eyes like other people my sisters and my mother cannot bear me, push me about from one corner to another, throw dish clouts at me, and only give me the scraps left over to eat. To-day they have given me so little that I am still quite hungry."

The wise lady replied, " Little Two-eyes, dry your face. I will tell you something, and that is you need not feel hungry any more. Just say to your goat :

'Little kid, bleat, bleat,
Little table, I would eat,'

76

and there will appear a freshly-laid table with delicious food on it, of which you may eat as much as you like. And when you are satisfied and do not require the table any longer, just say :

> 'Little kid, bleat, my dear,
> Little table, disappear,'

then it will vanish before your eyes." With that the wise woman went away.

Two-eyes thought, " I must try at once and see if what she says is true, for I am so hungry," and said :

> "Little kid, bleat, bleat,
> Little table, I would eat."

Hardly had the words been spoken before a table stood there covered with a little while cloth, and on it a plate, with a knife and fork and a silver spoon, and the most delicious eatables spread round, smoking and still hot as though they had just come from the kitchen.

Then Two-eyes said the shortest grace she knew, " The Lord make us truly thankful. Amen," and set to and ate heartily. When she had had enough she repeated what the wise woman had taught her :

> "Little kid, bleat, my dear,
> Little table, disappear."

The little table and everything on it at once disappeared. " That is a nice sort of housekeeping," thought Two-eyes, and was quite happy and cheerful.

In the evening when she came home with her goat, she found a little earthen bowl of food that the sisters had placed for her, but she did not touch it. The next day she went out again with her goat and left the few crusts set aside for her. The first and second time the sisters noticed nothing, but when it happened every time, they remarked upon it and said, " Something must be wrong with Two-eyes ; she leaves her food untouched every time, yet she used to eat up all that was provided for her ; she must have found some by other means."

In order to arrive at the truth of the matter One-eye resolved to accompany Two-eyes when she drove the goat out to the pasture, and to keep watch on her movements and see whether anyone brought her food and drink.

When Two-eyes was ready to start, One-eye stepped up to her and said, " I will go with you into the field and see that the goat is well tended and brought to a place where there is enough fodder."

But Two-eyes perceived what One-eye meant to do, and drove the goat out into the long grass, saying, "Come, One-eye, we will sit down together ; I want to sing you something." One-eye sat down, tired from the unaccustomed walk and the heat of the sun, and Two-eyes sang over and over again :

> " One-eye, are you waking?
> One-eye, are you sleeping?"

And then One-eye shut her eye and went to sleep. When Two-eyes saw that One-eye slept soundly and could not discover anything, she said :

> " Little kid, bleat, bleat,
> Little table, I would eat,"

and seating herself at her table she ate and drank till she was satisfied. Then she cried again :

> " Little kid, bleat, my dear,
> Little table, disappear,"

and everything disappeared immediately.

Two-eyes now awoke One-eye and said, " One-eye, you try to keep watch but fall asleep, while the goat might stray all over the place ; come, we will go home."

Then they went home and Two-eyes again left her little dish untouched. One-eye could not inform her mother why she would not eat, and gave as an excuse, " I fell asleep out of doors."

The next day the mother said to Three-eyes, " This time you must go and watch whether Two-eyes eats out

of doors, and whether anyone brings her food and drink,
for she must eat and drink secretly."

So Three-eyes stepped up to Two-eyes and said, " I
will go with you, too, and see whether the goat is well
tended and given enough fodder."

But Two-eyes saw her motive and drove the goat out
into long grass, and said, " We will sit down over there,
Three-eyes ; I want to sing you something." Three-eyes
sat down, tired with the walk and the heat of the sun,
and Two-eyes sang over again the same little song :

> " Three-eyes, are you waking ? "

But instead of singing as she ought :

> " Three-eyes, are you sleeping ? "

she sang from carelessness :

> " Two-eyes, are you sleeping ? "

and continued :

> " Three-eyes are you waking ?
> Two-eyes, are you sleeping ? "

Three-eyes then shut two of her eyes and slept, but the
third, to which the little rhyme was not addressed, did
not sleep. Three-eyes did indeed shut it, but only out of
cunning, as though it, too, was asleep ; but it blinked
and could see everything quite well. And as Two-eyes
imagined Three-eyes to be fast asleep, she said her little
verse :

> " Little kid, bleat, bleat,
> Little table, I would eat,"

then ate and drank to her heart's content, and afterwards
bade the table begone :

> " Little kid, bleat, my dear,
> Little table, disappear."

But Three-eyes had seen everything.

Two-eyes came up to her and awoke her, saying, " Ah, Three-eyes, have you been asleep ? You can watch well ! Come, we will go home."

When they got home, Two-eyes again ate nothing, and Three-eyes said to the mother, " I know now why the conceited creature does not eat : when she says to the goat out of doors :

> ' Little kid, bleat, bleat,
> Little table, I would eat,'

a table stands before her covered with delicious food much better than we have, and when she has had enough, she says :

> ' Little kid, bleat, my dear,
> Little table, disappear,'

and everything disappears ; I saw it all exactly. She sent two of my eyes to sleep with a little rhyme, but the one in my forehead fortunately kept awake."

Then the envious mother cried, " Do you want to fare better than we do ? You shall wish in vain for the future ! " She brought a butcher's knife, and stuck it into the goat's heart so that the creature fell dead.

When Two-eyes saw that, she went out full of sorrow, sat down on the ridge in the field and shed bitter tears.

At once the wise woman appeared again beside her and said, " Little Two-eyes, why do you weep ? "

" Have I not good reason to cry ? " she answered. " The goat that had my little table spread so nicely every day, whenever I repeated your little verse, has been killed by my mother ; now I must again suffer hunger and thirst."

The wise woman said, " Two-eyes, I will give you some good advice. Ask your sisters to give you the dead goat's entrails, and bury them in the ground in front of the house door, and it will bring you luck."

With that she disappeared, and Two-eyes went home and said to the sisters, " Dear sisters, give me just something from my goat ; I do not ask for anything good, only give me the entrails."

Then they laughed and said, " You may have that, if that is all you want."

Two-eyes took the entrails and buried them in the evening, when all was quiet, in front of the door, according to the wise woman's advice.

The next morning, when they all awoke and went out of the front door, there stood a wonderfully fine tree with leaves of silver and fruit of gold hanging between them, and there could certainly have been nothing more beautiful or costlier in the world. But they did not know how the tree had come there in the night. Only Two-eyes noticed that it had grown out of the remains of the goat, for the tree stood exactly on the spot where she had buried them.

The mother said to One-eye, "Climb up, my child, and take the fruit off the tree for us."

One-eye climbed up, but whenever she tried to take hold of one of the golden apples the branch slipped out of her hand; and this happened every time, so that she could not break off a single apple, try in whatever position she would.

Then the mother said, "Three-eyes, you climb up; you can look round better with your three eyes than One-eye."

One-eye scrambled down and Three-eyes climbed up, but Three-eyes was no more successful, and strive as she might the golden apples swung back.

At last the mother became impatient and climbed up herself, but could take hold of the fruit no better than could One-eye or Three-eyes, and always caught at the empty air.

Two-eyes then said, "I will go up; perhaps I shall fare better."

The sisters called out, "You, with your two eyes; what can you do?"

But Two-eyes climbed up, and the golden apples did not draw back from her; it was just as though they came towards her hands, so that she could pick off one after the other and brought down a whole apron full. The mother took them from her, and instead of treating poor Two-eyes any better, the mother and One-eye and Three-eyes were so jealous that she alone could pick the fruit that her lot was even harder than before.

It happened once that as they were standing together by the tree a young knight came by.

"Quick, Two-eyes," called the two sisters, "crouch down that we need not be put to shame by you," and hastily they threw over poor Two-eyes an empty barrel that stood by the tree, and thrust the golden apples she had been picking under it as well.

When the knight drew near, he turned out to be a handsome lord. He admired the splendid tree of gold and silver, and said to the sisters, "To whom does this beautiful tree belong? Whoever will give me a branch of it may ask what she likes for it."

One-eye and Three-eyes replied that the tree belonged to them, and they much wanted to break him off a bough. They each tried very hard, but could not do it, for the branches and fruit swung away from them at every effort.

Then said the knight, "It is indeed curious that the tree should belong to you and yet you have not the power to break off anything from it."

They persisted that the tree was their property; but while they were speaking Two-eyes let a couple of golden apples roll out from under the barrel, so that they ran along to the feet of the knight, for Two-eyes was angry at One-eye and Three-eyes for not speaking the truth. When the knight saw the apples he was astonished, and asked where they came from. One-eye and Three-eyes answered that they had another sister, but she did not let herself be seen, because she had only two eyes like any ordinary person. But the knight wanted to see her, and cried, "Two-eyes, come forward."

Thus encouraged, Two-eyes came from under the barrel, and the knight was astonished at her beauty and said, "You, Two-eyes, can doubtless break me off a branch from the tree."

"Yes," replied Two-eyes, "that I can well do, for the tree belongs to me," and, climbing up, she broke off a branch with its silver leaves and golden fruit, and handed it to the knight.

He then said, "Two-eyes, what shall I give you for it?"

"Ah!" answered Two-eyes, "I suffer hunger and thirst, sorrow and want, from early morn till late at night; if you would take me with you and deliver me, I should be happy."

The knight then lifted Two-eyes on to his horse and brought her home to his castle. There he gave her beautiful clothes, food and drink to her heart's content, and, because he was so fond of her, he was betrothed to her, and the wedding was held with great rejoicings.

When Two-eyes had been taken away by the handsome knight, the two sisters greatly envied her good fortune. "Yet we still have the wonderful tree," they thought, "even if we cannot break off any fruit from it, everyone will stop before it and come to us and spread the fame of it; who knows what we may reap!"

But by the next morning the tree had disappeared and their hopes with it; and when Two-eyes looked out of her little room, she saw to her joy that it stood outside and so had followed her there.

Two-eyes lived happily for a long time. Once two poor women came to her at the castle begging for alms. When Two-eyes looked into their faces she recognised her two sisters, One-eye and Three-eyes, who had fallen into such poverty that they were obliged to wander from door to door seeking their bread. However, Two-eyes bade them welcome and treated them well and cared for them, so that they both regretted from their hearts all the unkindness they had done to their sister in their youth.

The Shoes That Were Danced Into Holes

ONCE upon a time there was a King who had twelve daughters, each more beautiful than the others. They slept together in a hall, where their beds stood close together in a row, and every night when they lay in them the King locked and bolted the door.

In the morning, when the door was unlocked, he saw their shoes had been danced into holes, and it was a mystery how this had happened. The King issued a proclamation to the effect that whoever could find out how the shoes were danced into holes in the night should have one of the twelve sisters for his wife and succeed to the throne after his death, but whoever undertook to solve the mystery and had not done so in three days and three nights should forfeit his life.

Soon afterwards a Prince announced his readiness to attempt the solution of the problem. He was courteously received, and in the evening led into a room adjoining the hall. A bed was made up there and he was to watch who went in and danced in the sleeping apartment of the twelve sisters. Unfortunately, the Prince's eyelids soon felt heavy, and he went off to sleep ; when he awoke in the morning it was clear that all twelve sisters had been to a dance, for there were holes in all the shoes. The second and third night he fared no better, and his head was ruthlessly cut off.

After that several more princes and noblemen came, but all met the same fate and lost their heads. Then it happened that a poor wounded soldier was passing through the town, and when an old woman asked him what he was doing there he replied in jest :

84

" I have half a mind to offer myself as a spy on the twelve Princesses and see where they go to dance their shoes in holes every night, and then to become King for my trouble."

The old woman took him seriously and said, " It is not so difficult as you suppose ; all you have to do is not to drink the wine brought to you at night, and to sham being sound asleep." Thereupon she gave him a little cloak and said, " If you throw this over you, you will become invisible and can glide after the twelve maidens and see where they go."

The soldier, on hearing this advice, went in for the venture in good earnest and let himself be announced as a suitor. He was received with as much politeness as his predecessors and given royal raiment to put on. At bedtime he was led into the ante-chamber, and was getting into bed when the eldest daughter brought him a goblet of wine. He did not drink a drop of it, but let it all soak into a sponge he had tied under his chin. He then lay down and after a few minutes began to snore as if he were in a deep slumber.

The twelve Princesses heard his snores, and the eldest said, " He, too, might have spared his trouble and his life."

Then they got up, opened wardrobes, drawers, and boxes, out of which they took lovely dresses, and they decked themselves before their looking-glasses, skipping gaily about, overjoyed at the prospect of their dance.

The youngest seemed slightly depressed and said, " I don't know why you are all in such high spirits. I, for my part, feel as if some misfortune were hanging over us."

" You absurd goose," said the eldest. " What is there to be afraid of ? Don't you remember how many royal people have tried in vain to find out our secret ? I have given the soldier a sleeping draught like I gave the others, and you may depend the lout won't wake."

When they were all ready to start, they looked at the soldier and saw that his eyes were shut and that he lay perfectly still, so they imagined everything was all right.

The eldest went to the head of her bed and knocked on it ; immediately it sank through the floor, and they climbed down the opening one after the other, the eldest leading the way.

The soldier, who had watched their movements, now rose, flung on his cloak, and followed at the heels of the youngest. In the middle of the staircase he stepped on her dress, and she exclaimed in a great fright:

"Who is that? Someone caught hold of my dress."

"Don't be so silly," said the eldest. "You only caught it on a hook." And they went on till they reached the bottom. There they stood under a magnificent avenue of trees, the leaves of which were gold and silver, all flashing and gleaming.

The soldier thought, "You had better take a leaf as a witness," and broke off a twig.

The tree creaked, and the youngest sister called out. "Something is going to happen. Didn't you hear that noise?"

But the eldest again silenced her. "That was firing! Our Princes are firing salutes to welcome us."

And now they came to an avenue where all the trees had leaves of diamonds, and the soldier broke off a twig, and there was another tremendous crack.

The youngest sister jumped from fear, but the eldest insisted that the noises were only salutes.

Next they came to a lake on which twelve boats were at anchor, and in each was a charming young Prince. They were waiting for the twelve Princesses, and when they came they paired off together.

The soldier followed the youngest, and in a few minutes her Prince remarked, "How is it the boat seems so much heavier to-night? It is all I can do to move it."

"It is because the weather is so hot," suggested the youngest Princess. "I can hardly breathe."

On the other side of the lake stood a beautiful castle, brilliantly lit up, and from it came the sound of music. They all landed and entered together, and the couples danced, the soldier dancing invisibly, and whenever they stopped to refresh themselves with wine, he emptied the goblet just as they were lifting it to their lips.

This frightened the youngest Princess, but, as usual, the eldest silenced her. So they danced on till three o'clock in the morning, and by that time all their shoes were in holes, and they were obliged to leave off.

When they reached the staircase again, the soldier slipped in front and went back to bed ; and as the sisters, with lagging footsteps, tired and yawning, came into their apartment, he was already snoring as loudly as ever. They took off their lovely frocks, put them away, kicked their shoes under their beds, and lay down.

The next morning the soldier did not say anything ; but watched the same spectacle the second and third nights. Everything happened just the same, and the Princesses danced and danced till their shoes were almost in pieces.

The third time he took as evidence of what he had seen a goblet instead of a twig from the trees.

When the hour arrived when he was to go to the King he put the twigs and the goblet under his coat. The twelve girls stationed themselves behind the door to listen to what passed.

In answer to the King's question, " Where have my daughters danced their shoe s into holes during the night ? ' he replied :

" In an underground castle, with twelve Princes," and he produced his evidence.

Thereupon the King ordered his daughters to come before him, and asked whether the soldier spoke the truth. Seeing that they were found out and that it would be useless to deny anything, they confessed.

Then the King said, " Which of my daughters will you choose for your wife ? " and the soldier answered :

" As I am not so very young I'll have the eldest."

So their marriage was celebrated, and the soldier inherited the kingdom.

The Drummer

ONE evening a young drummer was walking by himself in the fields. He came to a lake, where he found on the bank three little bits of white linen. "This is very fine linen," he said, and put a bit in his pocket. He then went home, and without thinking any more about his find, lay down in bed.

Just as he was composing himself to sleep he fancied someone called his name. He listened, and then a low voice fell distinctly on his ear.

"Drummer, drummer, wake up!" it said.

The night was so dark that he could see no one, but he felt as if a figure were floating up and down at the bottom of his bed. "What do you want?" he asked.

"Give me back my garment that you took away last night from the shore."

"You shall have it," answered the drummer, "if you tell me who you are."

"Ah!" said the voice, "I am the daughter of a mighty King, but I am in the power of a witch, and I am banished to the glass-mountain. Every day I have to bathe in the lake with my two sisters, but without my garment I can't fly away again. My sisters have flown off long ago, but I am obliged to stay behind. I implore you to give it back to me."

"Be calm, child," said the drummer. "I will give it to you, of course."

He went and took the linen out of his pocket and handed it to her. She seized it eagerly, and turned to go.

"Wait a minute," said he, "perhaps I can help you."

"You can only help me," she replied, "by mounting the glass-mountain and delivering me out of the hands of the witch. But you couldn't possibly do it; even if you were quite close to the mountain you couldn't climb it."

"Where there is a will, there's a way," said the drummer. "I pity you, and fear nothing. But I don't know the way to the glass-mountain."

"The path lies through a forest inhabited by cannibals; that is all I may tell you," she answered. And then he heard her flit away.

At daybreak the drummer got up, slung on his drum, and went fearlessly into the cannibal forest. After he had gone a little distance he looked round, but saw no giants. He thought, "I must wake up the sluggards," and he beat a tattoo on his drum which frightened the birds.

In a few minutes a giant who had been lying in the grass reared his huge form, and stood there as tall as a pine-tree. "You rascal!" he exclaimed, "what do you mean by beating your drum and waking me out of my beauty sleep?"

"I am beating the drum," he answered, "because a thousand men are coming behind who want to know the way."

"What are they doing in my forest?" asked the giant.

"They intend, for one thing, to kill you, and cleanse the forest from all such monsters."

"Oh, indeed," said the giant. "I'll trample them dead like so many ants."

"Do you think you could catch them?" said the drummer, with a sneer. "If you stooped to pick up one he would be off like a shot and hide himself, and if you lay down to sleep hundreds would creep out of the bushes and climb on your body; and as they are all armed with steel hammers they would make short work of beating in your skull."

The giant grew sad, and thought. "It is difficult to know how to deal with these small, cunning folk. With wolves and bears I am at home, but I am at a loss what to do with earth-worms."

"Look here," he said aloud, "if you, little fellow, will go away now, I promise I will never molest you and your comrades in future, and if you have any particular wish that I can fulfil, tell me, and I will see what I can do for you."

"You have long legs," said the drummer, "and can

run faster than I. Carry me to the glass-mountain, and I will signal to my men to retreat and leave you in peace."

"Come here then, little worm," said the giant, "seat yourself on my shoulder, and I will carry you wherever you want to go."

The giant lifted him, and the drummer began to play his drum from sheer joy. The giant thought this was the signal for the others to withdraw.

After a time a second giant stood in the path, who took the drummer away from the first giant and put him in his button-hole. The drummer held on to the button, which was as big as a dish, and still felt in quite good spirits.

Then they came to a third giant, who took the drummer out of the other's button-hole, and put him on the brim of his hat. The drummer walked up and down, and could see away over the tree-tops. Catching sight of a mountain in the blue distance, he thought to himself, "That is the glass-mountain for certain," and it was. The giant had only to take a few strides to get to the foot of it.

When the giant put him down, the drummer desired him to carry him to the top, but the giant muttered something in his beard, and went back to the forest. There stood the poor drummer in front of the mountain that was so high; it was like three ordinary mountains, one on top of the other, and as transparent and smooth, besides, as a mirror. He did not know what to do. He tried to climb, but in vain, for he always tumbled back.

As he stood there, not knowing how he should act, he caught sight of two men fighting. He went up to them, and saw that the bone of contention was a saddle lying on the ground.

"What fools you are," he said, "to quarrel about a saddle when you have no horse to put it on."

"The saddle is worth quarrelling about," replied one of the men. "If anyone sits on it, and wishes himself somewhere, even at the end of the world, he'll be there in a jiffy. The saddle is our joint property. It is my turn to ride on it, but he will not let me."

"I will settle the dispute," said the drummer. He went a few paces off and stuck a white pole into the ground.

Then he came back, and said, "Now then, run to the pole, and who reaches it first will have first right to the saddle."

Both started, but they had not run many steps before the drummer swung himself into the saddle and wished himself at the top of the glass-mountain. In a twinkling he was there.

An old stone house stood on the very top, in front of which was a large fishpond, and beneath it a dense, dark wood. He did not see a sign of man or beast. All was silent except for the rustling of the trees. The clouds seemed very close over his head.

He knocked at the door of the house, but not till he had knocked three times did an old woman with a brown face and pink eyes open it. She had spectacles on her long nose, and scanned him sharply. Then she asked what his business was, and he asked for board and lodging. "You shall have it," replied the old lady, "if you work for it. I will set you three tasks."

"Why not?" said the drummer. "I don't shirk work, and I don't care how hard it is."

The old woman then admitted him, giving him a good supper and a comfortable bed.

In the morning she took a thimble from her shrivelled finger, and, handing it to the drummer, said: "Take this thimble and with it bale out the water in the pond till there isn't a drop left. The work must be completed by night, and all the fish arranged according to their kind and size on the bank."

"A curious task," thought the drummer. He went to the pond and began to bale. He worked hard the whole morning, but what was the good of trying to empty a great sheet of water with a thimble? It would take a thousand years at least. At dinner-time he gave it up as a bad job, saying to himself, "It is all the same whether I work or not."

Then a maiden came out of the house and placed a basket of food before him. "How sad you seem!" she said. "Is anything the matter?"

He looked at her and saw she was very beautiful. "Alas!" he exclaimed, "I cannot perform the first task she has given me. How shall I ever be able to perform the other two ? I came here to seek a Princess, but I have not seen her yet."

" Wait here," said the girl ; " I will help you. You are tired ; lay your head in my lap and sleep, and when you wake the thing will be done."

The drummer was only too charmed to obey.

Directly his eyes closed the girl twisted a wishing-ring, and exclaimed, " Water, come up. Fish, come out."

The water immediately rose like a white mist and mingled with the other clouds, and the fish jumped on to the bank and arranged themselves in order of size and colour.

When the drummer awoke he saw with amazement what had happened.

The girl said, " One of the fish is not lying by his fellows, but is quite alone. If the old woman comes this evening to see if all has been done as she ordered, she will at once say, ' What is this fish doing here?' Then throw the fish in her face, and say, ' It is for you, old witch.' "

At evening, when the old woman came and asked the question, he threw the fish in her face. She stood as if she did not notice the insult and said nothing, but her eyes blinked wickedly.

The next morning she remarked, " Yesterday you had too easy a time ; I must give you harder work. To-day you must cut down the whole wood, cut up the timber, arrange it into faggots, and everything must be ready by the evening." She gave him an axe, a hatchet, and two saws, but they were all made of lead.

He did not know what to do, but the maiden arrived at dinner-time with his food, and said, " Lay your head in my lap, go to sleep, and when you wake the work will be finished."

She twisted her wish-ring on her finger, and the whole wood collapsed with one fearful crackle, as if invisible giants had been felling it.

He awoke, and the girl said, " Look! the timber is all severed and arranged in faggots. Only one branch lies apart ; when the old woman comes to-night, take it and give her a blow with it, and say, ' That's for you, old witch.' "

The old woman came. " You see," she said, " how very

easy is the work I give you. But what is that branch doing there ? "

He took it up and gave her a bang with it, saying, " That's for you, old witch." But she appeared not to feel it and only laughed mockingly.

" To-morrow," she said, " you shall collect all the faggots, pile them up, and set fire to them."

He rose at dawn and began to collect the wood, but how was it possible for a single man to gather a whole forest ? He made no progress. Well for him that the girl did not leave him in the lurch ! She brought his dinner, and when he had eaten it he put his head in her lap and went to sleep. On waking, the whole vast mass of timber was alight, the flames reaching to the sky.

" Listen," said the girl, " when the witch comes she will impose on you again. Do what she asks you without fear, so that you give her no cause for complaint. If you are the least bit afraid, she will seize you and pitch you into the furnace. When you have done as she bids you, you can end by catching hold of her and throwing *her* on the flames."

The girl departed, and the old witch came. " Fire ! I am freezing ! " she exclaimed, " but that nice fire will warm my old bones. But look, there's a log that won't burn ; fetch it out. If you can do that, you are free to wander where you please, so jump in gaily."

The drummer did not hesitate a moment and sprang into the flames ; they did not even singe his hair. He dragged out the log and laid it down. Hardly had it touched the earth then it changed into the charming girl who had helped him out of his difficulties, and by the golden draperies she now wore he knew she was the Princess.

The old woman laughed. " You think," she jeered, " that you've got her, but I tell you, you haven't yet."

She was in the act of rushing at the girl to take her away, when the drummer seized the old woman with both hands and flung her into the fire.

The Princess then looked critically at the drummer, and having duly considered that he was certainly a handsome youth who had risked his life for her sake, she held out her hand, and said, " You have dared everything for me. Promise to be my true love, and I will marry you."

She led him into the house and showed him great chests and cupboards, filled with the treasures the witch had accumulated. They left all the gold and silver and only took the precious stones.

As they did not wish to linger on the glass-mountain any longer, she said to him, " I have only to turn my wishing-ring and we shall be at home."

" All right," said the drummer, " wish us in front of the city gates."

In a second they were there, and the drummer said, " First I will go to my parents and tell them the news. Wait for me here in this field and I will soon be back."

" Ah ! " cried the Princess, " I implore you to be careful. On no account kiss your parents on the right cheek, else you will forget everything."

" How could I possibly forget you ? " he said, and gave her his right hand and promised that he would soon return.

When he entered his old home no one knew him, he was so altered, for the three days he had spent on the glass-mountain had really been three years.

Then he revealed who he was, and his parents in their delight fell on his neck, and he was so touched that he kissed them on both cheeks, forgetting the maiden's injunction. Directly he had kissed the right cheeks of his parents all thought of the Princess left him. He emptied his pockets, and laid handfuls of pearls and diamonds on the table. The parents did not know what to do with all this wealth.

At last the father built a superb castle, surrounded by gardens, fields and woods, fit for a Prince to live in. And when it was ready the mother said to the drummer, " I have chosen a bride for you, and we will fix the wedding for this day week." The son expressed himself content.

The poor Princess meanwhile had waited a long time in the field before the city gates. When evening came, and he did not return, she felt convinced that he had kissed his parents on the right cheek and forgotten all about her. Her heart was heavy, and she wished herself in a lonely forest-house and not at her father's court. Every evening she walked into the town and passed the drummer's house ; many times the youth saw her without knowing her again. At last she heard people saying, "To-morrow, he is to be married." And she thought, "I will make an effort to win him back."

On the first day of the wedding festivities she twirled her ring, and said, "I want a dress that shines like the sun." At once the garment lay before her, and looked as if it had been woven out of sunbeams.

When the guests were assembled she entered the hall. Everyone was struck by the beauty of her dress, especially the bride herself, who had a passion for fine clothes. She went up to the stranger and asked if she would sell her gown.

"Not for money," was the answer, "but if I may linger all night beside the door of the room in which the bridegroom is going to sleep, I will give you the dress with pleasure."

The bride could not resist the offer, and consented to the arrangement, but first she mixed the bridegroom a sleeping-draught with his wine, which sent him into a deep slumber.

When the house was quiet the Princess crouched before the door of the sleeping apartment, opened it a little, and called :

> "Drummer, drummer, listen to me.
> Have you forgotten me quite ?
> Did you not sit beside me on the mountain height ?
> Did I not save you from the witch's wiles ?
> And you plighted your troth with smiles ?
> Drummer, drummer, listen to me."

But it was no use ; the drummer did not wake, and when morning dawned the Princess was obliged to own herself unsuccessful and go away.

The second evening she turned her ring, and said, "I want a dress as silver as the moon."

When she appeared in draperies as soft and filmy as moonbeams, she again excited the envy of the bride, who accepted the dress as a present and granted the wearer permission to spend another night outside the bridegroom's door.

In the stillness of the night she called again to the drummer, but as he was stupefied by the sleeping-draught he did not waken, and in the morning the Princess went sorrowfully back to her forest-house.

But some of the servants in the house had heard the strange girl's sad lament and told the bridegroom about it ; they told him that he must have heard it if he had not been drugged with the sleeping-draught that had been mixed with his night-cap.

The third evening the Princess turned her ring, and said, " I want a dress that flashes like the stars."

When she appeared at the ball the bride was in ecstasies over the new dress, and said, " I must and will have it," and the owner consented to give it to her on the same condition.

This time the bridegroom did not drink the wine on retiring to rest, but poured it under the bed. When all the house was still he heard a soft voice saying :

> "Drummer, drummer, listen to me.
> Have you forgotten me quite ? "

Suddenly his memory returned. " Ah," he cried, " how faithless and cruel I have been ! But the kiss which in the joy of my heart I pressed on my parents' right cheek is really to blame." He jumped up, took the Princess by the hand, and led her to his parents' bedside. " Here is my true bride," he said ; " if I marry the other I shall do her a great wrong."

The wedding festivities began over again, and the first bride was allowed to keep the three lovely dresses as compensation, and expressed herself satisfied.

The Golden Goose

ONCE there was a man who had three sons. The youngest, called Dunderhead, was mocked and ridiculed by the other two, and on every opportunity slighted and despised. Once it happened that the eldest brother wanted to go into the forest to hew wood, and his mother gave him a delicious egg-pancake and a bottle of wine to take with him as refreshment.

When he reached the forest he met a little grey-haired old man, who wished him good day, and said, "Give me a piece of cake out of your wallet and a sip of wine; I am terribly hungry and thirsty."

The clever son answered, "Why should I give you my cake and wine, and have none for myself? Take yourself off!" and he passed by the old grey-haired man with contempt.

When he began to chop a tree he soon made a false stroke, and the axe struck his arm instead of the timber, so that he was obliged to go home and have the arm bound up.

The second son then went out to the forest, and his mother gave him, as she had given the eldest, a pancake and a bottle of wine. He, too, saw the grey-haired little man, who begged from him a morsel of cake and a sup of wine. But the second son said brusquely, "I am not going to rob myself to feed you," and passed on, leaving the little man standing with outstretched hands. He, too, met his punishment, for instead of hitting the tree he hit his own leg, and had to be carried home.

Then the dunderhead said, "Father, let me go out and hew wood."

His father answered, "Look what harm your brothers have done themselves by going. You understand nothing about it, and had better leave it alone."

The dunderhead, however, begged so earnestly that at last his father consented.

His mother gave him for lunch a cake cooked in the ashes, with water and a bottle of sour beer.

When he came into the forest he saw the little grey-headed old man, who greeted him and said, " Give me a bit of your cake and a drink of your wine."

The dunderhead replied, " Sit down ; I have nothing but a cake cooked in the ashes, and sour beer, but we will eat and drink together if you like."

So they sat down, and as the dunderhead produced his ash cake it turned into an egg-pancake, and the sour beer turned into good wine.

After they had eaten and drunk, the little man said, " Because you have a kind heart, and have shared your meal with me, I will do you a good turn. Over there stands an old tree ; cut it down, and you will find something worth having in its trunk."

The dunderhead went and cut down the tree, and as it fell a goose flew out, with feathers of real gold. He picked it up and went to an inn to pass the night. The landlord had three daughters, who were curious when they saw the wonderful goose, and longed to possess one of its gold feathers. The eldest thought, " Probably I shall have an opportunity of plucking one out," and when the dunderhead had gone out of the room she caught hold of the bird by its wings, but she could not withdraw her hand, for her fingers were stuck fast. A moment later her sister came in with the idea of taking a feather, but she had scarcely touched her sister before she was stuck fast too. Then the third sister appeared, and though the others shouted out, " For Heaven's sake, don't come here," she rushed up to see what they were doing, and remained sticking fast ; so all three of them had to pass the night with the goose.

The next morning the dunderhead took up his goose and departed, not troubling himself about the three girls hanging on behind. They were forced to trot at his heels, sometimes to the right, sometimes to the left.

In the middle of the fields they met the pastor, and when he saw the little procession he said, " Aren't you ashamed of yourselves, you bold, forward hussies, to run after a young fellow over the fields in this fashion ? " Whereupon he seized the youngest by the hand and tried to draw her back, but could not free himself, and so had to run on with the rest.

In a few minutes they met the sexton, who looked astounded at seeing the parson following at the heels of three girls. He called out, " Mr. Parson, where are you off to at such a rate ? Don't forget there is a christening to-day." Then he ran up to him and caught him by the sleeve and, like the others, was stuck fast, and had to follow too.

As the five progressed one behind the other they met two labourers coming out of the hayfields with their rakes. The parson shouted to them to set him and the sexton free. But scarcely had they touched the sexton than the labourers, whether they liked it or not, had to hook on ; so that there were now seven people following the dunderhead and his goose.

They came to a town where lived a King who had a daughter who was so serious that no one had ever succeeded in making her laugh. Therefore the King had declared that anyone who could make her laugh should marry her.

The dunderhead, when he heard this, went into the Princess's presence with his goose and suite, and when she saw the seven people hanging on to each other, one behind the other, she began to laugh so loudly there was no stopping her.

The dunderhead then asked for her hand in marriage, but the King was not disposed to favour his suit. He raised endless objections and said that before he could consent to have him for a son-in-law he must bring him a man who could drink a whole cellar of wine.

The dunderhead bethought him of the little grey old man, and went to the place in the forest where he had cut down the tree. There the little man was, seated with a very distressed face. The dunderhead asked what was the matter.

He answered, " I am consumed with such a terrific thirst. Nothing will quench it. Cold water I cannot

G

endure. I have already emptied a cask of wine, but what good is such a drop in wetting a parched stone?"

"Listen, I can help you," said the dunderhead. "Come with me and you shall slake your thirst."

He led him into the King's cellar, and the little man went to the great barrels and drank and drank till his sides hurt, and by the end of the day he had emptied the cellar.

Again the dunderhead demanded the hand of the Princess, but the King was angry with the fellow whom everyone gibed at for his stupidity, and imposed new and harder conditions. He must now bring a man to the court who could eat up a mountain of bread.

The dunderhead again went to the place in the forest where he had cut down the tree.

There sat a man with a painful expression of countenance, lacing his body in with straps. "I have eaten a whole bakery full of rye bread," he said, "but what is that when one suffers from such great hunger as mine? My stomach is empty, and, to prevent myself from dying of starvation, I must pull myself in like this."

The dunderhead rejoiced greatly, and said, "Get up! I will show you how you can eat and be filled." He led him to the court, where they had collected all the flour in the kingdom to bake an enormous mountain of dough.

The man from the forest set to work and ate with such a will that in a day the whole structure had disappeared.

A third time the dunderhead demanded his bride, but once more the King tried to get out of the bargain.

This time he asked to see a ship that could sail on dry land as well as on sea. "Sail up in it," he said, "and you shall have my daughter for your wife."

Without further delay the dunderhead departed again for the forest, and found the old grey-headed little man, who said, "I have drunk for you and eaten for you, and now I will provide you gladly with the ship. I have done all these things for you because you were kind to me."

So he gave him a ship which sailed by land and sea, and when the King saw it he could no longer refuse to give the dunderhead his daughter.

The wedding was celebrated, and, after the King died, the dunderhead inherited the throne and reigned well.

The Boy Who Learnt to Shudder

A FATHER had two sons, of whom the elder was clever and quick, and knew how to set about everything; but the younger was stupid, and could not understand or learn anything, and when people saw him they said, "He'll be a trouble to his father yet!"

When anything was to be done the elder son always had to do it; but if his father told him to go, late in the evening, or perhaps at night, to bring anything and his way lay through the churchyard, or any other gruesome place, he would answer: "Oh, father, I'm shuddering!" for he was afraid.

In the evening, when they were telling stories round the fire that made the hearers' flesh creep, some among the audience would say, "It makes me shudder!" On these occasions the younger son would sit in a corner listening to their talk, and could not imagine what they meant; and he often exclaimed, "They all say, 'I'm shuddering! I'm shuddering!' *I* never shudder; I suppose it must be some art that I don't understand."

One day his father said to him, "Listen, you fellow in the corner there, you're growing a great sturdy lad; so you must learn something by which you may earn your bread. See what pains your brother takes to learn; but upon you good counsel seems lost."

"Indeed, father," replied the son, "I'm quite willing to learn something; and if it could be managed, I should like to learn to shudder; for I don't know how to do that at all."

The elder brother laughed when he heard this speech, and thought to himself, "My patience, what a stupid fellow that brother of mine is; he'll never do any good all his life, for a bit of iron must be bent early if it's to be a hook." The father sighed, and answered, "You'll learn to shudder in time, I'll warrant; but you will never earn your living by it."

Soon afterwards the parish clerk came to their house to visit them; then the father told him his troubles, and complained how his younger son was an ill-disposed lad, who knew nothing and would learn nothing. "Just fancy," he said, "when I asked him how he intended to get his bread he said he should like to learn to shudder."

"If that's all he wants," answered the clerk, "he can soon learn; let him come with me; I'll polish him off for you."

The father had no objection; for he thought, "At any rate, the boy will be improved a little." So the clerk took the boy home, and he was set to toll the church bell.

A few days afterwards the clerk woke the lad at midnight, and told him to get up and go into the church tower to ring the bell. "I'll teach you what it is to shudder," thought he, and went secretly before. When the boy got up into the belfry, and turned round to grasp the rope, he saw a white figure standing on the stairs, opposite the window.

"Who's there?" he cried; but the figure gave no answer, and never stirred.

"Answer me!" cried the boy, "or be off with you; you've no business to come here at night!"

But the clerk remained motionless, for he wanted to make the lad believe he was a ghost.

The boy asked a second time, "What do you want here? Speak, if you're an honest fellow, or I shall fling you downstairs."

The clerk thought, "He does not mean that"; so he did not utter a sound, but stood motionless, as if he had been hewn out of stone.

Then the lad called to him a third time. When that too proved vain, he took a run, and gave the ghost such a push that it tumbled down ten stairs, and lay motionless in a corner. Then he rang the bell, and returned home, going to bed without a word to anyone, and falling fast asleep.

The clerk's wife meanwhile waited for her husband a long time, but he did not return. At last she became alarmed, woke up the boy, and asked: "Do you know where my husband is? He went up into the tower before you."

" No," answered the boy ; " but some fellow stood on the stairs opposite the window ; and as he would neither answer me when I called to him, nor go away, I thought he was a rogue, and flung him downstairs. If you go and look you will see if it was your husband ; but I shall be very sorry if it is."

The woman ran off, and found her husband, who was lying in a corner, groaning and lamenting, for the fall had broken one of his legs.

She carried him home, and then ran with loud cries to the lad's father. " Your boy," she declared, " has been the cause of a great misfortune ; he has flung my husband downstairs in such a way as to make him break his leg ; pray rid our house of that good-for-nothing."

The father started when he heard this ; he came running to the clerk's house, and began scolding his son soundly. " What wicked tricks are these ? " he cried ; " the spirit of mischief must have possessed you."

" Father," pleaded the boy, " I'm quite innocent ; just listen to me. He stood there in the night as if he had come for some bad purpose. I did not know who it was, and called to him three times telling him either to speak or to go away."

" Ah ! " said the father, " you only cause me sorrow and woe ; get out of my sight ; I will not look at you any more."

" Very well, father," answered the lad, " only wait till it is day, then I'll go and learn to shudder. I shall at least know an art by which I may earn my living."

" Learn whatever you like," said the father, " it's all the same to me. Here are fifty dollars for you ; go out into the world, and don't tell anyone where you came from, or who is your father, for I am ashamed of you."

" Well, father, it shall be as you wish," answered the youth ; " if you ask no more than that, the thing's easily done."

When day came the lad put his fifty dollars in his pocket, and went out into the highroad. And as he walked on he kept repeating to himself, " If I could only shudder ! if I could only shudder ! "

Soon there came up a man, who heard what the boy said. When they had gone on a little way, and came in sight of a gibbet, he said to the boy, " See, yonder is a tree where seven robbers have been hung, all together. Sit down there and wait till night comes, and you'll learn how to shudder."

" If that's all I have to do," replied the youngster, " it's easily done ; and if I really learn to shudder so quickly you shall have my fifty dollars ; come again to-morrow morning."

The lad went to where the gibbet stood, sat down under it, and waited till evening. And because he was cold he lighted a fire ; but at midnight the wind blew so cold that in spite of the fire he could not keep warm. As the wind swung the corpses to and fro, so that they rattled against each other, he thought, " If I am cold down here by the fire, what must it be for those poor fellows up there ? " And because he had a kind heart, he placed a ladder, mounted, unfastened the dead robbers one after another, and brought all the seven down. Then he poked up the fire, blew it into a blaze, and set them all round, that they might warm themselves. But they lay there and never stirred, even when the fire caught their clothes. So he said : " Take care what you're about, or I shall hang you up again." But the dead robbers did not hear him ; they remained silent, and let their rags burn on.

Then he became angry, and said : " If you won't take care I can't help it, but I won't be burnt with you " ; and he hung them up again, all in a row. Then he sat down again by his fire and went to sleep.

The next morning the man came to him, and wanted his fifty dollars. " Well," he said, " you know what it is to shudder, I fancy ? "

" No," replied the young man ; " how should I know ? Those poor fellows up there never opened their mouths, and were so stupid that they would have let their few miserable rags of clothes burn."

Then the man saw that he would not win his fifty dollars that day ; so he went away, saying, " I never met such a fellow in my life."

The lad continued his journey, and began again to mutter to himself, " If I could only shudder ! if I could only shudder ! "

A carter who came striding along behind heard this, and asked, " Who are you ? "

" I don't know," answered the lad.

The carter asked again, " Where do you come from ? "

" I don't know."

" Who's your father ? "

" That I may not tell you."

" And what is it you keep muttering to yourself ? "

" Why," answered the boy, " I should like to learn to shudder, but no one will teach me how."

" Leave your foolish talk," said the carter, " and go with me. I will get a lodging for you somewhere."

The youth went with the carter ; and in the evening they came to an inn, where they resolved to pass the night. As they came into the room, the lad said again, quite loudly, " If I could only shudder ! if I could only shudder ! "

The host, who overheard him, laughed, and observed, " If you want to do that, you may find a good opportunity here."

" Be quiet, do," said his wife : " many a foolhardy man has lost his life there already. It would be a pity for his handsome eyes if they should never see the daylight again."

But the youth said, " If it were ever so difficult, I would learn, for that's why I have come out " ; and he would not let the host rest till he had told how there was an enchanted castle, not far off, where a man might easily learn what it was to shudder, if he would only stay there for three nights. The King had promised his daughter in marriage to anyone who would attempt it ; and she was the most beautiful young maiden on whom the sun shone. And in the castle there were concealed great treasures, guarded by evil spirits, which treasures would then come to light, and might make a rich man of a very poor one. Many had gone into the castle, but no one had come out again.

The next morning the lad went to the King and said, " If I might be permitted, I should be glad to watch for three nights in the enchanted castle."

The King looked at him, and, liking his appearance, replied, " You may do so ; and you may ask for three things, which you can take into the castle with you ; but they must be lifeless things."

" Then," answered the lad, " I shall ask for a fire, a

carpenter's bench, and a lathe, with the knife that belongs to it."

The King caused what he wanted to be carried into the castle the same day. When night was coming on the lad went up and made a bright fire in one of the rooms, put the carpenter's bench and the knife beside it, and sat down by the lathe. " If I could only shudder ! " he said ; " but I shall not learn even here."

Towards midnight he wanted to make up his fire ; as he was blowing at it, he heard voices suddenly crying from one of the corners, " *Me-ow, me-ow,* how cold we are ! "

" You blockheads," said he, "what are you mewing about ? If you are cold, come and sit by the fire and warm yourselves."

When he had said that, two great black cats came bounding up with a leap, and sat down, one on each side of him, looking at him wildly with their fiery eyes. After a while, when they had warmed themselves, they said to him : " Comrade, will you have a game at cards with us ? "

" Willingly," replied he, but first show me your paws " ; and they stuck out their claws towards him.

" Why, what long nails you have ! " he cried ; " wait a moment, I'll cut them for you."

With that, he took them by the neck, lifted them on to the carpenter's bench, and screwed their paws into it. " I don't care about playing cards with you," he said, " now that I've seen your fingers " ; and he killed them, and threw them out into the water.

But as soon as he had silenced these two, and was about to sit down again beside his fire, there came from every hole and corner black cats and black dogs, dragging red-hot chains ; there came more and more, so that he could not hide himself ; and they shrieked horribly, and trod upon his fire, pulled it to pieces, and wanted to put it out. For a time he bore their antics quietly ; but when they became too bad, he took up his turning-knife, and crying, " Away, you rabble ! " began hacking at them right and left. Some ran away ; the rest he killed and threw into the pond outside.

When he came back, he blew the embers of his fire into a blaze and warmed himself ; as he sat thus, his eyes would not keep open any longer, and he felt a great desire to sleep. Looking round, he saw a great bed standing in the corner. " That's just what I want," he said, and laid himself down upon it. But just as he was going to close his eyes, the bed began to move, and began rolling through the whole castle.

" Go on, that's right," he cried ; " go on as fast as you please." And the bed went rolling on as if six horses were drawing it, over thresholds and staircases, up and down. All at once, " crack, crack," it turned topsy-turvy, so that it lay upon him like a mountain. But he flung the mattresses and pillows away, got up, and said, " Whoever likes, may ride now," and lay down by his fire and slept till day.

In the morning the King came ; and when he saw the youth lying upon the ground, he thought the ghosts had killed him, and that he was dead. And he said, " It's a pity, for he is a handsome young fellow."

The boy heard this, and jumped up, saying, " It's not so far with us yet ! " The King was astonished and pleased, and asked him how he had fared.

" Very well," he answered. " One night has passed ; the others will pass too."

When the boy went back to the inn, the host opened his eyes in wonder. " I did not think I should see you again alive," said he. " Have you learned what it is to shudder ? "

" No," he answered, " it has been all in vain. I wish anyone could tell me what it is ! "

On the second night he went up again into the old castle, sat down by his fire, and began his old song, " If I could only shudder ! "

When it was nearly midnight he heard a noise and tumult, at first distant, then louder and louder, and then there was a short pause, after which half a man came tumbling down the chimney and fell close to him. " Hallo," he cried, " there's half a one still wanting—this isn't enough ! "

Then the noise began again ; there was a great tumult and uproar, and the second half came tumbling down too. " Wait a bit," he said ; " I'll blow up the fire a little."

When he had done that, and looked round again, the two halves had joined together, and a man of hideous aspect was sitting in his place.

"I didn't mean it in that way," cried the lad; "that bench is mine."

The man wanted to push him away, but the boy would not allow it, thrust him aside forcibly, and sat down again in his place. Then more men came falling down; they brought with them nine great bones and two skulls, and set up the bones to play skittles with. The youth thought he would like to play too; and he said, "Listen, may I make one?"

"Yes," answered they, "if you have money."

"I've money enough," he rejoined, "but your balls are not round"; and he took the skulls and put them into his lathe, and gave them a turn.

"So," he cried, "they'll bowl much better; now we'll be merry!"

He played with them, and lost some of his money; but when twelve o'clock struck everything vanished from his sight; and he lay down quietly and went to sleep.

When the third night came, he sat down again upon the bench, and said crossly, "If I could only shudder!"

Suddenly there entered a man who was taller than any he had yet seen, and had a horrible appearance; he was an old man, with a long white beard.

"Oh, you wretch!" he cried, "now you shall soon learn how to shudder! for you shall die!"

"Not so fast," replied the youth; "if I'm to die, I must first give my consent."

"I'll soon make an end of you," roared the apparition.

"Softly, softly," retorted the youth, "don't be too boastful; I fancy I'm as strong as you are, and stronger too."

"We'll see that," cried the old man, "if you're stronger that I am, I will let you go; come, we will try it."

He led the youth through dark passages to a place where there was a smith's forge; the old man took an axe, and with one blow struck one of the two anvils into the earth.

"I can do more than that," said the youth, and he went to the other anvil. The old man stood by to watch him, with his white beard hanging down. Then the young man seized the axe and not only split the anvil at a blow, but wedged the old man's beard tightly into it.

"Now I have caught you," he cried, "and it's your turn to die!"

Then he snatched up a bar of iron, and battered away at the old man till he whimpered and begged him to leave off, promising him great riches if he would hold his hand. So the young man pulled out the axe and released the old man's beard.

The old man led him back into the castle and showed him three great chests full of gold. "One of these," he said, "is for the poor, one for the King, and the third for you."

As he said this the clock struck twelve, and the spirit vanished, leaving the youth standing alone in the dark.

"I shall manage to get out of this," he said; and he groped about till he found his way to his room, and went to sleep by his fire.

Next morning the King came again, and said, "I fancy by this time you've learned what it is to shudder?"

"No, indeed," replied he; "what can it be? A bearded old man came, and showed me a great deal of gold; but he did not tell me what it was to shudder!"

"Well," said the King, "you've disenchanted the castle and you shall marry my daughter."

"That's all very pleasant," answered he, "but I don't know yet what it is to shudder!"

Then the gold was brought up, and the marriage was celebrated. But though the young man was very happy, and loved his wife very much, he could not avoid saying, "If I could only shudder! if I could only shudder!" At last the young wife grew angry about it, and her chambermaid said, "I will find a remedy for it; he shall learn to shudder after all."

So he went to the brook which flowed through the garden, and had a whole pailful of little gudgeon brought in. And she told her mistress to wait till her husband was fast asleep at night, and then draw the coverlet from him, and pour the water with the gudgeon over him, so that the little fishes sprang all about.

Then the young man woke up, and cried: "I'm shuddering—hu—hu—what makes me shudder? Dear wife, now I know what it is to shudder!"

The Wise Griffon

ONCE upon a time there lived a King, but where he reigned and what was his name I don't know. He had no sons, but an only daughter, who was always ill, and no doctor knew how to cure her.

Someone foretold that if the King's daughter ate a certain sort of apple she would get well. So the King issued a proclamation to the effect that anyone who would bring an apple to the Princess that would restore her health, should marry her.

A peasant who had three sons said to the eldest, " Go into the orchard, pick a basketful of our choicest apples, and take them to the castle. Perhaps they will make the Princess well again. Then you marry her and become King."

So the son gathered the apples and went to the castle. On the way he met an old man, who inquired what he had in his basket.

Ulrich replied, " Frogs."

The man said, " So be it," and went on.

When Ulrich came to the castle he asked the porter to let him through the gates, as he had brought a hamper of apples which he thought would cure the Princess. The King, when he heard this, was delighted, and summoned Ulrich to his presence. But, unfortunately, when the hamper was opened it was found to contain nothing but frogs. The King was exceedingly angry, and had Ulrich turned out of the castle immediately. Ulrich went home and told his father.

Then the peasant dispatched his second son, whose name was Sam, but he did not meet with success either. He came across the same old man, who asked him what he had in his basket, and Sam replied, " Crabs."

When he came to the castle Sam told the porter he had brought a basket of apples which were certain to cure the Princess.

The porter replied that they had been deceived once, and it was not likely they would be deceived again.

But Sam declared so positively that there was nothing but apples in the basket, that they let him in at last. The basket was then opened in the King's presence, and was found to contain crabs. The King was furious, and had the man horsewhipped and turned out of the castle.

Sam went home and told his father of his experience.

The peasant's youngest son, who was nicknamed " Stupid Hans," now asked his father if he might go to the castle with a basket of apples.

" You, indeed ! " exclaimed his father. " A pretty man to send ! If your brothers failed, it is not likely you will succeed."

But Hans persisted in asking to be allowed to go.

" You stupid fellow," said the father, " wait till you grow a little brighter. For the present leave me in peace."

He turned away impatiently, but Hans went after him, pulled his coat-tails, and said, " Father, I want to go very much ; do let me go."

" All right, get along with you," said the peasant ; " but I am sure you will not do better than the others, and worse if possible."

The boy was so delighted at having gained permission that he skipped and capered about.

" Doesn't this silly behaviour show what a fool you are ? " said his father. " You are even more silly than I thought."

But Hans was not in the least put out, and went to bed looking forward with joy to the morning. He did not sleep much, but when he did he dreamed of beautiful Princesses, splendid castles, and gold and silver.

He got up early in the morning, picked the apples, and started for the castle. He met the same little man the others had met, who asked him what he had in his basket. Hans answered promptly, " Apples, to cure the Princess."

And the little man said fervently, " So be it."

Of course, when he came to the castle Hans was not
welcomed, and everyone was sceptical of there being apples
in his basket.

" Two men have been here," they told him, " and insulted
the King by bringing frogs and crabs."

Hans assured them he would not deceive the King for
the world, and that he had really brought a basket of the
best apples that grew in the whole kingdom. Hans had
such an honest face and spoke so earnestly that it was
impossible to suspect him of telling a lie. He was admitted,
and when the King opened the basket there indeed was
a quantity of rosy, tempting apples. The King was overjoyed, and took some at once to the Princess. After she
had eaten two or three the servants came and told the
King she was cured. Almost immediately afterwards his
daughter came herself. She told him that directly she
had eaten a bit of one apple she had jumped out of bed
perfectly well again.

The King was delighted, but after all was loth to give
Hans his daughter's hand at once. " You must first make
me a boat," he said, " which will sail as well on dry land
as on water."

Hans said he would certainly make the boat, and went
home and related everything.

The old peasant at once sent Ulrich into the woods to
make the required boat. Ulrich set to work confidently,
whistling and singing.

About midday, when the sun was at its hottest, he saw
approaching the little old man he had met on the road
when he was carrying his apples to the King.

" What are you making there ? " he asked.

Ulrich answered, " Wooden spoons," and went on making
what he thought was a boat, but when he had finished he
found nothing but a pair of wooden spoons.

The following day Sam went, and everything happened
to him as it had happened to Ulrich.

On the third day Stupid Hans was allowed to go. He
worked hard, and was very cheerful over it. At midday,
when the sun shines most powerfully, the little man
appeared and asked him what he was about.

" Making a boat that will sail on dry land as well as on

the water; and if I can do it I shall marry the King's daughter perhaps, and be King."

"So be it," said the old man.

At sunset the boat was complete, and Hans sailed in it to the town.

The King saw him coming, but still hesitated about letting him marry the Princess.

Hans was now asked to keep watch over a hundred hares from early morning till late at night. If he lost one of them he would lose the Princess.

Hans started at once with his hares, and as he took such good care not to let one out of his sight, a servant was sent from the castle to ask him for a hare. The excuse was that visitors had come unexpectedly and the hare was wanted for dinner.

But Hans saw it was a trick, and said, "Tell the King to have a hare served to-morrow instead of to-day."

The servant was, however, unwilling to depart without the hare, and Hans said at last, "If the Princess will come herself I will give her a hare."

When the servant had gone the little man appeared again and asked Hans what he was doing.

"I am keeping watch over a hundred hares," was the answer, "and if I lose one I shall not be allowed to marry the Princess."

"Take this whistle," said the little man, "and if a hare escapes, whistle and it will come back instantly."

When the Princess came Hans gave her the hare and put it in a kerchief for her. She had not carried it a hundred yards when Hans whistled, and the hare wriggled out of the handkerchief and ran back.

Before night came, Hans whistled again to see if all the hares were there, and then drove them to the castle.

The King was much surprised at this proof of Hans being able to look after a hundred hares without losing one. Yet he still declined to let him marry the Princess till he had done something else. This time he was to bring him a feather out of the Wise Griffon's tail.

Hans started off to fetch it. At night he came to a castle, for in those days there were no inns. He saw the master of the castle, and asked to be put up for the night.

When he was asked where he was going, he said, " To the Wise Griffon."

" Oh, indeed," answered the man, " you are going to the Wise Griffon, are you ? I have been told he is an oracle and knows everything. I have lost the key of my money-box. Will you be so kind as to ask him where I am to find it ? "

" With pleasure," said Hans.

Early in the morning he started off. That night he put up at another castle. When the people staying there heard he was on his way to the Wise Griffon, two of them told him their daughter was ill and they had tried in vain to cure her. Would he kindly ask the Wise Griffon for a prescription to make her well ?

Hans promised and went off. He came to a lake where, instead of a ferry boat, a big, strong man was employed to carry people across to the other side of the water. The man asked Hans where he was travelling to.

" To the Wise Griffon," answered Hans.

" Well, if you find him," said the man, " just ask him why I have to carry people across this water."

" All right," said Hans, " I will ask him."

The man took him over the water, and after that he soon reached Wise Griffon's castle, but the bird was not at home ; only his wife was in. She asked him what he wanted.

Hans told her everything. First, he wanted a feather out of the Wise Griffon's tail ; secondly, he wanted to know where the lost key of a cash-box was ; thirdly, he was to ask for a prescription for the daughter of the two guests at the castle ; and lastly, he wanted to be told why the big, burly man at the ferry had to carry people over.

The wife said, " No one can ever get a word in edgeways with the Wise Griffon, my good friend ; he rates everybody. But if you like to try, you may hide under his bed, and when he is sound asleep pull a feather out of his tail. About the other matters I will ask him myself."

When the Wise Griffon came in at night he said, " Wife, I smell someone in the room."

" You are right," replied the wife. " A man has been here, but he went away just now."

The bird then said no more.

At midnight Hans heard the bird snoring loudly, so he ventured to pull out a feather.

Suddenly the bird woke up and exclaimed, "Wife, I certainly smell a human being, and I am sure I felt some-one pull my tail."

The wife responded, "You must have been dreaming. There *was* a man, as I told you, here, but he went away. He talked about a key to a cash-box which had been lost, and which no one knew where to find."

"Oh, the pack of idiots!" exclaimed the Wise Griffon; "the key is under a log in the wood-house, behind the door."

"He also said something about some parents who had a sick child they couldn't cure."

"Oh, the fools!" exclaimed the Wise Griffon; "in the cellar under the stairs a bird has made a nest of her hair. If she gets her hair back she will recover."

"The man said something, too, about a big, burly fellow carrying people across a ferry, and he wanted to know why he was obliged to do it."

"Oh, the stupid blockhead!" said the bird; "if only he would carry someone as far as the middle and there leave him he need never carry anyone else over."

In the morning the Wise Griffon got up and went out. Hans crept from his hiding-place and was in high glee at having obtained his feather and all the information he wanted.

But the wife repeated over again what the bird had said, so that he should be sure not to forget, and then Hans started.

First of all he came to the man at the water, who inquired what answer he had brought him from the Wise Griffon.

Hans replied, "Take me across the water, and I will tell you."

The man carried him to the other side, and then Hans told him that if he dropped someone into the middle he need never carry anyone else over.

The man was pleased and said he would carry Hans over again to show his gratitude, but Hans said, "No, thank you; I am on the right side and content to stay there."

H

Then he arrived next at the castle where the people were whose daughter was ill.

Hans showed them the cellar, and the bird's nest was found, and when the hair was restored to her, the girl jumped out of bed quite well. Her father and mother overwhelmed Hans with presents and thanks.

He started off a rich man, and when he came to the castle where they had lost the key he went straight into the wood-house and found it for them.

The master of the castle was so charmed to get it back that he gave Hans a handsome reward.

When Hans put in an appearance before the King with all his presents and money, the King asked enviously where he had got them all.

Hans told him the Wise Griffon had given him everything, and then the King thought he should like to make the Wise Griffon's acquaintance himself. He set out, but when he came to the ferry was dropped into the middle of the water and drowned.

Hans married the Princess and became King.

The Goose-Girl at the Well

THERE was once an old, old woman, almost as old as the hills, who lived with her flock of geese in a wilderness between two mountains, where she had a small house.

The wilderness was surrounded by a dense forest, and every morning the old woman took her crutches and stumped into the forest. Here she was more active than you would have imagined such a very old woman could be. She gathered grasses for her geese, picked as many wild berries as she could reach with her hands, and carried all home on her back.

One morning a fine young fellow came tramping through the forest. So far he had met no one, and then suddenly he saw the old crone kneeling on the ground mowing her grass with a sickle. She had stuffed a large bundle in her satchel and two baskets stood near filled with wild pears and crab-apples.

"Mother," said he, "you'll never be able to carry all that."

"I must carry it all, pretty gentleman," she said. "Rich people's children wouldn't need such things. But the poor peasant has a saying, 'Be careful of the odds and ends.' Would you like to help me?"

The young man felt sorry for the old woman. "My father is no peasant," he said. "I am the son of a rich Count; but to show that it is not only peasants who can carry burdens I will take your bundle."

"If you'll only try," said the old woman, "I shall indeed be grateful. It's about an hour's walk, and you'll have to take the pears and apples too."

The young Count was a little dismayed when he heard what the distance was, but the old woman was not going to let him off. She bound the bundle of grass on his back and slung the baskets on his arm.

"You see," she said, "how easy it is."

"No," replied the Count, "it is not easy," and his expression became pained; "the bundle is as heavy as if it were chock-full of rocking-stones, and the apples and pears are as weighty as if they were made of lead."

He wanted to free himself of his burdens in a few minutes, but the old crone would not allow him to rest.

"Look now!" she exclaimed in a mocking voice, "the fine young gentleman can't carry what an old woman has borne on her back a hundred times."

So long as the way lay over level ground he could endure, but when they came to the mountain-side and had to climb, and the loose stones rolled under his feet as if they were alive, his strength was almost exhausted. Perspiration poured off his brow and shivers ran down his back.

"Mother," he said, "I can't go on. I must rest a little."

"Nothing of the kind," said the relentless witch; "when we get home you shall rest, not before. So push on; the exercise will do you a deal of good."

"You shameless old hag!" exclaimed the Count, and tried to throw off the bundle, but in vain, for it was so firmly fastened to his shoulders that it might have grown there.

The old woman laughed heartily at his attempts and danced around him on her crutches.

"Don't lose your temper, pretty sir," said she. "Carry your bundle patiently, and when we get home I'll give you your reward."

What could he do? He was obliged to trudge on and resign himself to the old creature's tyranny. She seemed to grow more and more nimble, while he was weighed down more than ever. Once, with a spring, she leapt on to the top of the bundle, and though she was shrivelled and thin as a broomstick her weight exceeded that of the most buxom peasant girl. The youth's knees trembled and bent under him, but the old woman drove him on with a switch and with kicks on the legs. Under pressure, he arrived at last at the old woman's house, ready to drop from fatigue.

When the geese saw the old woman they spread their

wings, craned their necks, and flew towards her, crying, " Wulle ! wulle ! " Behind the flock came a strapping lass with a stick in her hand. Tall and muscular, she was as ugly as darkness itself.

The old woman now clambered down from her perch and relieved the Count of the bundle and the baskets. She looked at him with quite friendly eyes and said in a pleasing tone, " Sit down on that bench, and you shall have the reward and refreshment you have so honestly earned."

Then she turned to the goose-girl and said, " Go into the house, dearest daughter ; it won't do for you to be alone with a young, good-looking gentleman ; he might fall in love with you."

The Count hardly knew whether to laugh or to cry. " Such a beauty as that ! " he thought, " Even if she were thirty years younger I shouldn't look at her."

Meanwhile the old woman caressed and stroked her geese as if they had been babies, and then followed her daughter into the house.

The youth stretched himself on a bench in the shade of an apple-tree. The air was soft and cool. Round him stretched a green meadow thickly carpeted with cowslips, wild thyme, and a thousand other flowers.

" It is very charming here," the Count said, " but I am so tired I cannot keep my eyes open, I'll take a nap."

After he had been asleep a short while the old woman came and shook him.

" Get up," she said. " You mustn't stay here. I've given you a bad time of it, truly, but it hasn't cost you your life. Here's your reward. You are in no need of money or land, so I give you this." She handed him a small box, carved out of an emerald. " Take care of it," she said, " it will bring you happiness."

The Count sprang to his feet, conscious that his weariness had fled and that he was as strong and fit as ever. He thanked the old woman for her present, and without turning his head to get another glimpse of the fair daughter he departed.

The Count wandered for three days before he found the way out of the wilderness. Then he came to a great town, and as no one knew him he was led to the royal castle, where the King and Queen sat on the throne. The Count dropped on one knee, drew out the emerald box, and laid it at the feet of the Queen.

She bade him rise and give the knick-knack into her hands. Scarcely had she opened it and looked inside than she fell to the ground in a dead faint.

The Count was instantly taken into custody and led to prison.

Thereupon the Queen opened her eyes and cried, "Let him come back." Then she ordered everyone to go away and leave her to have a private conversation with the stranger.

When the Queen was alone with him she began to cry bitterly. "Of what avail is all this pomp and splendour when every morning I wake up full of care and sorrow? I have had three daughters, the youngest of whom was a miracle of loveliness. She was as white as snow, as pink as apple-blossom, and her hair shone like sunbeams. When she cried she shed tears that were pearls and precious stones. The King, when she was fifteen years old, ordered all three daughters to come before the throne. You should have seen the admiration of the courtiers when the youngest came in; it was like the sun rising. The King said, ' My daughter, I do not know when my end may come, but I will decide to-day what each of you shall have at my death. You all love me, but the one of you who loves me the most shall have the largest share.' Each daughter said she loved him best. ' Cannot you express,' asked the king, ' how much you love me, and then I shall be able to judge?' The eldest said, ' I love my father more than sweet honey'; the second, ' I love my father more than my prettiest frock.' But the youngest was silent. 'And you, my dear child,' asked her father, 'how much do you love me?' ' I do not know,' she answered, 'and cannot compare my love with anything.' But the King insisted that she must mention something. So she said at last, ' The best dishes have no flavour without salt. I love my father as much as I love salt.' When the King heard this answer he became furious, and said, 'If your love for me resembles nothing better than salt it shall be rewarded with salt.' Thereupon he divided his kingdom between the two elder daughters, but the youngest, with a sack of salt tied to her back, was led into the wild forest by two servants and left there alone. Soon afterwards the King repented his severity and harshness, and sent people out to look for her in the forest, but she was nowhere to be found. Imagine my feelings when I opened the emerald box to see a pearl lying in it exactly like one of my daughter's tears. Please tell me how you came by this treasure."

The Count related how the old woman in the wood had given it to him. He believed her to be a witch. Of the Queen's lost daughter he had heard and seen nothing.

The King and Queen then resolved to look up the old woman, for they naturally thought that in the quarter the pearl had come from news of their child might be gleaned.

The old woman was sitting in her house in the wilderness, spinning. It was already dark, and a log on a smouldering hearth gave but a feeble light. Suddenly there was a fluttering and cackling without, and the geese were driven home from the meadow. In a few minutes her daughter came in. The old woman scarcely noticed her, and shook her palsied head. The daughter sat down, took her spinning-wheel too, and made it hum, as young women do, the threads flying. Thus they sat together for two hours without speaking a word.

At last something rattled the window and two fiery eyes glowered through the pane. It was an old screech-owl, and its " Tit wit-hoo " made the old dame look up and say, " Now, daughter ; it's time ; go out to your work."

The daughter stood up and went out. Where did she go ? Over the meadows, on and on till she came to the valley. She stopped by a well where three oak-trees grew. The moon meanwhile had risen in a great silver ball over the mountains. It was so light you could have found a pin. The girl drew a mask from her face and began to wash in the well. When she had finished, she threw the skin she had washed off in the water and lay down on the grass to dry in the moonlight. You never saw such a transformation. Instead of a mud-coloured plait, gold locks like sunbeams broke loose from the girl's head and

spread round her till they enveloped her whole figure like
a mantle. Her eyes shone through her tresses like stars
in the sky, and her cheeks bloomed with the soft pink of
apple-blossom.

But the beautiful maiden was sad ; she sat down and
cried bitterly, and one tear after another splashed through
her hair on to the ground. There she sat, and would have
sat a long time had not the bushes crackled and snapped
behind her. She sprang up like a deer at the sound of
the sportsman's shot. Just then a black cloud covered
the moon, and the girl again slipped into the old dark skin
and disappeared like a light blown out by the wind.

Trembling all over like an aspen leaf, she ran into the
house again. The old woman stood at the door, and the
girl was going to tell her what had happened when the
witch laughed gaily and said she knew all about it. She
went into the parlour and threw on another log. But
she did not sit down again to her spinning-wheel, but
fetched a broom and began to sweep and dust.

" Everything must be clean and tidy," she remarked
to the girl.

" But, mother," said the girl, " why do you begin work
at such a late hour ? What's going to happen ? "

" Don't you know what time it is ? " asked the old
woman.

" Not quite midnight," answered the girl. " Not much
after eleven."

" Have you not thought," went on the old woman,
" that it is three years to-day since you came to me ?
Your time is up ; we cannot stay together longer."

The girl looked frightened, and said, " Oh, dear mother,
don't cast me out. Where shall I go ? "

The old woman did not wish to reveal to the girl the
fate in store for her. " I haven't long to stay here,"
she said, " but before I leave, the house must be cleaned
thoroughly ; so don't interrupt me in my work. You
needn't be afraid, you will have a roof over your head,
come what may, and the reward I am going to give you
will be ample for your wants. Go to your room, wash off
your dark skin, put on the silk dress you wore when you
came here, and then wait till I call you."

But now we must go back to the King and Queen, who, accompanied by the Count, had gone into the wilderness to look for the old woman. The Count in the forest got separated from them, and had to go on alone. The next day he thought he was on the right path, and walked on and on till night fell; then he climbed a tree where he intended to sleep, for he was afraid he might lose his way in the dark.

When the moon rose and lit up the landscape he saw a figure coming down the mountain. He recognised the same goose-girl (though she had no stick in her hand) that he had seen in the old woman's garden.

But how astounded was he when he saw the girl go to the well, take off her skin, wash, and let down her beautiful golden tresses! He had never seen anyone so beautiful in his life. He scarcely dared breathe, but stretched out his head as far as it would go from his bower of foliage to gaze at her. Perhaps he stretched too far, for the bough he was on snapped, and at the same moment the lovely apparition hastily resumed her old skin, and fled like a deer. And as just then a cloud came over the moon, he lost sight of her.

The minute after she had vanished, the Count came down from the tree and followed the direction she had taken. He had not gone far before he saw the King and Queen, who had seen the light shining from the window of the old woman's house and were making for it. The Count told them of the wonderful transformation he had witnessed by the well, and they were sure the beautiful girl must be their lost daughter.

In great glee they continued their way, and soon came to the old woman's little house. The strangers looked in at the window and saw the old woman at her spinning-wheel. The little parlour was as spick and span as if the little fairymen lived there who cannot bear a speck of dust on their feet. The King and Queen summoned up courage and knocked softly on the window-pane.

The old woman appeared to expect them. She got up, and exclaimed in a friendly tone, "Come in; I know who you are!"

When they had walked into the parlour the old woman

said, "You might have spared yourselves this journey if three years ago you had not unjustly spurned your child, who is so good and lovely. But you really did her no harm after all. For three years she has tended my geese, and in that time her pure heart has remained unsullied. But the anxiety you have suffered on her account has long ago punished you enough." Then she went to the bedroom door, and called, "Come out now, dear little one."

The door opened, and the Princess appeared in her silken draperies, with her golden hair and shining eyes, and complexion like apple-blossom. She embraced and kissed her father and mother, and all of them wept for joy.

The young Count stood by, and when she saw him she blushed, she knew not why, till she looked like a moss-rose.

The King then said, "My child, I have now bequeathed my kingdom to the others. What shall I give you?"

"She needs nothing," the old dame interposed. "I will give her the tears she has shed for you. They are priceless pearls, more beautiful than those found in the sea, and worth more than a hundred kingdoms. And in reward for her services I shall make her a present of my little house."

As the old woman said this the walls creaked a little, and the old woman vanished before their eyes. On looking round, they saw the small dwelling had changed into a magnificent palace, and a long table stood ready laid, with flunkeys running hither and thither.

There is more of the story, but my grandmother, who told it to me, had not a good memory, and she had forgotten the rest. I have an idea that the beautiful Princess was married to the Count, and that they lived together in the fairy palace happy and content.

Whether the white geese who were fed in the pasture by the little house were maidens whom the old woman had brought home with her at one time or another, and were now changed back into human beings again, as maids of honour to the young Queen, I do not know, but I think it probable. One thing is certain, the old woman was not a wicked witch at all, but a wise woman who meant to do good. Most likely it was she who at the Princess's birth endowed her with the gift of shedding pearls instead of tears.

The Three Spinning-Women

THERE was once an idle girl who would not spin.

At last, one day, the mother lost all her patience, so that she beat the girl, who began weeping aloud. The Queen was just driving by, and when she heard the crying she stopped her carriage, came into the house, and asked the mother why she beat her daughter. The woman was ashamed to expose her daughter's idleness; so she said: "I cannot get her away from the spinning-wheel, and I am poor, and cannot provide the flax."

The Queen answered: "There is nothing I like so much as spinning; let your daughter go with me into the palace. I have flax enough, and she shall spin as much as she likes."

The mother consented with all her heart, and the Queen took the girl with her.

When they came to the castle, she led the girl upstairs and showed her three rooms, which were filled with the finest flax from floor to ceiling. "Now spin me all this flax," she said, "and when you have spun it all you shall marry my eldest son."

The girl was alarmed in her secret soul, for if she had worked every day from morning till evening, till she grew to be three hundred years old, she could not have spun all that flax. When she was left alone she began to cry, and sat thus for three days without stirring a finger. On the third day the girl did not know what to do, and went sadly to the window. There she saw three women approach. The first of the three had a broad splay foot; the under lip of the second was so big that it hung down to her chin; and the third had an immensely broad thumb to one of her hands. The three stopped below the window, looked up, and asked the girl what was the matter. She told them of her distress. "If," they said, "you will invite

us to your wedding, and not be ashamed of us, but call
us your cousins, and let us eat at your table, we will spin
the flax for you."

"With all my heart," replied the girl.

She let in the three singular women, and they sat down
and began to spin. The girl hid the three spinning-
women from the Queen; and every time she came showed
her the quantity of thread that had been spun off; so
that the Queen could not praise her sufficiently.

Then the three women took their leave, saying to the
girl: "Do not forget what you promised us; it will be
for your happiness."

When the girl showed the Queen the empty rooms, and
the great heap of spun thread, the Queen made arrange-
ments for the wedding.

"I have three cousins," said the girl, "and as they
have done me many kindnesses, I should not like to be
forgetful of them in my prosperity; permit me to invite
them to our wedding, and let them sit at table with us."

The Queen and the Prince consented. When the
marriage day came, the spinning-women arrived, most
comically dressed, and the bride said to them: "Welcome,
dear cousins."

"How is it," asked the Prince, "that your friends are
so ugly?" Then he turned to the one with the great
splay foot, and asked: "How came you to have such
a broad foot?"

"From treading the wheel," she replied.

Again the bridegroom went to the second, and asked:
"How came you by that hanging lip?"

"From moistening the thread," she replied.

Then he asked the third: "Why is your thumb so
broad?"

"From twisting the thread," she replied.

Then the Prince was alarmed, and declared: "My
beautiful bride shall never touch a spinning-wheel again."

So she got rid of the distasteful employment.

The Twelve Brothers

ONCE upon a time a King and Queen lived happily together, and had twelve children, every one of them a boy. The King said one day to the Queen: "If our thirteenth child happens to be a girl I shall have the twelve lads put to death, in order that my riches and kingdom shall be hers alone." The mother, of course, was very sorrowful, and mourned the whole day.

Her smallest son, who was always with her, and whom she called Benjamin, said: "Mother, why are you so sad?"

"Dearest child," she answered, "I mustn't tell you."

But he would give her no peace till she did so.

Because she cried so much her son comforted her. "Don't cry, dear mother," he said; "we will save ourselves and go away."

"Yes," she urged. "Go with your eleven brothers into the forest, and one of you climb to the top of the highest tree you can find and keep watch. Look at the tower of the castle. If the baby proves to be a son a white flag shall fly there, and you may all come back, but if it is a daughter I will order a red flag to be hoisted, and then fly for your lives, and may God protect you."

After she had blessed her sons they all set out for the forest. They took it in turns to climb the highest oak tree and keep watch.

When eleven days had passed it was Benjamin's turn, and he saw there was a flag flying on the tower; it was, however, not the white, but the blood-red, flag that announced their death-sentence.

The brothers were very angry, and said: "Why should we suffer death for the sake of a girl? We swear to be revenged; wherever we find a girl she shall shed blood."

Thereupon they went deeper into the forest, and found in the very middle, where it was thickest, a little enchanted cottage that stood empty. "Here," said they, "we will live, and you, Benjamin, being the youngest and weakest, shall stay at home and keep house while we procure food."

The brothers lived thus in the cottage for ten years and the time went quickly.

The little daughter the Queen had borne grew up, and her heart was as kind as her face was lovely. She wore a gold star on her forehead. Once when there was a great wash going on she saw hanging out to dry twelve shirts, and she asked her mother whose shirts they were, as they would be much too small for her father.

The Queen answered with a sigh: "Dearest, they belong to your twelve brothers."

"My twelve brothers?" said the maiden. "How is it I have never seen or heard of my twelve brothers? Where are they?"

"God knows!" replied the Queen; "they are wandering about in the world."

And she related how the King had threatened to kill all his sons when his daughter was born.

"Ah, dear mother, don't cry," said the daughter when the Queen had finished her story. "I will go and look for my brothers."

She took the twelve shirts and set off for the forest. She wandered the whole day, and towards evening arrived at the enchanted cottage. She walked in and found a boy there, who asked where she came from and where she was going.

"I am a King's daughter," she explained, "and I am looking for my twelve brothers." She then showed him the twelve shirts.

Benjamin saw at once that this was his sister, and he said, "I am your youngest brother Benjamin!" They both began to cry for joy and kissed and hugged one another.

"Dear sister," said Benjamin, after a while, "there is one thing to be considered. We have entered into an agreement to kill every girl we meet, because a girl was the cause of our leaving our kingdom."

Then she said: "I don't mind dying if through it I can save my brothers."

"No," he answered, "I'll see that you don't die. Sit under this vat till the eleven brothers come in, and then we will arrange matters."

She did as he told her, and at nightfall the others came back from the chase. As they sat round the table and ate their supper, one of them asked:

"Is there any news to-day?"

"Well," said Benjamin; "promise before I begin that the first girl we meet shall not be killed."

"Yes," they consented at once, "we promise she shall be spared. Now, tell us the news?"

"Our sister is here!" said Benjamin, and lifted the vat. The King's daughter came forward in her royal garments, with the gold star on her forehead, looking delicate, gentle, and beautiful. They were all delighted, fell on her neck and kissed and caressed her, and loved her dearly.

Now she stayed at home with Benjamin and helped with the house work.

There was a small garden belonging to the enchanted cottage, in which grew twelve tall lilies, which were also called students, and the sister, thinking they would make pretty buttonholes for the brothers, picked them to lay by their plates at the table. But no sooner had she plucked the flowers than the twelve brothers were changed into twelve ravens and flew away out of the forest. The cottage and garden, too, both disappeared. So the poor child was left alone in the wild forest, and as she looked round she saw an old woman standing near.

"My child," said the old woman, "what did you do that for? Why didn't you leave the twelve white flowers alone? They were your brothers, who are now changed for ever into ravens."

"Oh," said the girl, tears rolling down her cheeks, "can nothing be done to change them back?"

"No," said the old woman, "nothing in the world except one thing, and that is difficult, for if you would release them you must keep dumb for seven years. You must neither speak nor laugh, and one hour in which the rule is broken will make the rest in vain. If you speak a single syllable it will be the death of your brothers."

Then the girl said in her heart: "I know I shall release my brothers." She went and sought a high tree, climbed to the top of it and sat there and span. She neither spoke nor laughed.

It happened that a King, who one day was hunting in the forest, beheld the beautiful King's daughter, seated in the tree, with the gold star on her forehead, and was so charmed that he called up and asked if she would become his bride. She gave no answer, but nodded her head slightly.

Then he climbed up the tree, carried her down, placed her on his horse, and rode home. The marriage was celebrated with great rejoicing, but the bride neither spoke nor laughed.

When they had lived a few years happily together, the King's mother, who was a wicked woman, began to slander the young Queen. She said to the King:

"I believe you have brought home a vulgar beggar-wench as your wife. If she is really dumb and can't speak, she might at least laugh. Anyone who can't laugh must have a bad conscience."

The King would not listen at first, but his mother was so persistent, and made up so many scandalous stories about the Queen, that at last he was talked over, and allowed his wife to be condemned to death.

A huge fire was kindled in the courtyard, in which the Queen was to be burnt. She was already bound to the stake, and the flames were licking her dress with red tongues when the very last moment of the seven years expired. A fluttering and whirring sound was heard in the air overhead, and down fell twelve ravens. Directly they touched the earth they turned into the twelve brothers, who were no longer bewitched. They scattered the fire, extinguished the flames, and, freeing their beloved sister, took her in their arms and kissed her over and over again. Now that she might open her lips and speak, she told the King why she had been dumb and had never laughed. The King was very glad that her innocence was proved, and they all lived happily till the end of their lives.

The wicked mother-in-law was brought before the judge, who sentenced her to a terrible death she had well deserved.

Cocky and Henny

SAID little Cocky to little Henny, "It's the season for nuts, just now; suppose we go up on the hill and have a good feast before the squirrel carries them all away?"

"Very well," answered little Henny, "come along— we'll go and enjoy ourselves together."

So they went together to the mountain; and because it was a sunshiny day they stayed there till the evening. Now I don't know whether it was because they had eaten so much or that they had grown proud, but they would not go home on foot. So Cocky had to make a little carriage of nutshells; and when it was ready Henny took her seat in it, and said to Cocky, "Now, you may harness yourself to it."

"That's a good joke," cried Cocky. "I'd rather walk home at once than harness myself to your coach; I didn't mean to do it that way. I don't mind being the coachman, and sitting on the box, but as to pulling, I couldn't think of it."

They were still disputing the point when a duck came running up and quacked: "You thieves, you, who gave you leave to come among my nut trees? Wait, it shall be the worse for you"; and so saying she began to attack Cocky. But Cocky was not idle in the matter—he ran at the duck, in his turn, and gave her such a dose of kicks with his spurs that she cried out for mercy, and was glad enough to allow herself to be harnessed to the carriage as a punishment. So now Cocky took his seat on the box as coachman, and they went off at full-speed, Cocky crying to the duck to run as fast as ever she could.

They had gone some distance when they met two foot-passengers—a pin and a needle. These two began crying out to them to stop, urging that it would be so dark directly that they would not be able to go a step further. They also complained of its being dreadfully dirty on the road, and begged for a lift in the carriage, as they had been in the tailors' house-of-call, and had remained sitting later than usual over their beer. Cocky, considering that they were slender people, who would not take up much room, let them both get in; but made them promise that they would not tread on Henny's toes.

Late in the evening they came to an inn ; and as they did not care to go any further that night, and the duck, moreover, was not strong on her legs, but kept waddling from side to side, they put up there. The host at first made many objections, and declared that his house was full—the truth was, he thought his guests were not people of very high quality ; but as they were very smooth-spoken, and promised him he should keep the egg Henny had laid on the way, and have the duck into the bargain, who laid one every day, he consented to let them stay there for the night. So they ordered the best cheer he had in the house, and made quite a merry night of it.

Next morning, when it was only just daybreak, and every one was fast asleep, Cocky woke up Henny, brought out the egg, and pecked it open. They ate it together, and threw the shell on the hearth. Then they went to the needle, who was still asleep, and took him by the head and stuck him into the cushion of the host's chair ; the pin they stuck into his towel ; then they ran off across the heath as fast as they could. The duck, who preferred sleeping in the open air, and had therefore remained in the yard all night, when she heard them scuttling off, roused herself, and soon found a brook on which she swam away, a good deal more quickly than she had run before the carriage.

A couple of hours later the host got out of bed, and, having washed his face, went to dry it with the towel ; the pin scratched his face right across, and made a red line from his right ear to his left. Then he went into the kitchen, and set about lighting his pipe ; and when he came to the hearth the egg-shell flew up in his eyes. " Everything seems to fly at my head this morning," he grumbled, and sat down in a bad humour, in his arm-chair ; but he jumped up in a great hurry, and cried, " Oh, dear ! " for the needle had pricked him worse than the pin ; and this time the pain was not in his head. Now he was completely angry and suspected the guests who had arrived late the evening before. But when he went to see after them they were gone. Then he swore that in future he would have no ragamuffins in his house, who eat much, pay nothing, and play you tricks into the bargain.

The Poor Little Peasant

THERE was once a village full of rich people, with only one poor man among them, and he was called the Little Peasant. He had not so much as a cow, still less money to buy one with; and he and his wife wanted a cow very badly indeed. Once he said to her, "I have a good idea; there is Gaffer Schreiner, you know. Why shouldn't he make us a calf out of wood, and paint it brown, so that it looks like any other calf; in time, it would grow up and bear us a cow."

The wife approved of the plan, and Gaffer Schreiner hammered and planed them a calf, painted it and made its head move, so that it could be lowered and look as if it were chewing grass.

The next morning when the cows were being driven out, the peasant called in the cowherd, and said, "Look here, I have a calf so small that it must be carried."

The cowherd replied, "Very good," carried it out into the meadow, and set it down in the middle of the grass.

The little calf stood as if it were eating, and the cowherd said, "By the way it eats, it ought to be able to walk." When evening came, and he was preparing to drive the flock home, he said to the calf, "If you can stand there all this time eating, you can find your way home on your own four legs, and I needn't have the trouble of carrying you."

The peasant stood at his door waiting for his calf. When he saw the cowherd driving his herd through the village, he asked him why the calf was not there.

"Oh!" said the cowherd, "your calf insisted on standing where it was and eating, instead of coming home."

"But I must have my little calf," said the peasant; "come and show me where to find it."

So the two set out together for the meadow, but when they got there the calf had been stolen.

"It has run away," said the cowherd.

"I don't believe it," replied the peasant, and he brought the cowherd before the constable for his negligence. The cowherd was ordered to give the peasant a cow in compensation for the loss of his calf.

Now the peasant and his wife possessed the cow they had so long wished for, they were glad from the bottom of their hearts, but as they could not afford to feed it properly it soon had to be slaughtered. They salted the meat, and the peasant went into the town to sell the skin in order to buy a calf with the proceeds. On the way he saw a raven, with broken wings, sitting on a windmill. Out of compassion he took it and wrapped it in the cow skin, but rain came on, and such a storm blew up, that he abandoned his expedition and went into the mill and asked for shelter.

The miller's wife was alone in the house and said to the peasant, "Lie down on that straw." Then she brought him some bread and cheese.

The peasant ate and lay down with his skin beside him. The woman thought, "He is dead tired, and will sleep."

The priest at this moment came to call, and she said, "My husband is out, so we will banquet together."

The peasant pricked up his ears, and when he heard the word "banquet," thought it was rather too bad that he should have been put off with bread and cheese.

Soon the woman was busy laying the table with roast meat, salad, cake and wine. Just as the pair were going to sit down, there was a knock outside and the woman exclaimed, "Good gracious! there's my husband." With all speed she hid the roast meat in the coal scuttle, the wine under the pillows, the salad in the bed, the cake under the bed, and the priest in the linen-press outside in the passage. Her husband came in and remarked that the weather was so bad he thought another flood was coming. She said, "Thank God, you are safe home again!"

The miller then saw the peasant lying on the straw, and asked, "Who is that fellow?"

"Oh!" replied the woman, "that is a poor tramp who

asked for shelter from the storm, so I gave him bread and cheese and said he might lie there."

The husband said, " I have no objection, make haste and get me something to eat."

" There is nothing but bread and cheese," replied his wife.

" I shall be content with anything, only let me have it quickly," replied the miller. Then, looking at the peasant, he shouted, " Come and have a bite with us."

The peasant did not wait to be invited twice; he stood up and came to the table.

" What have you there ? " the miller asked, when he saw the skin with the raven in it.

" I have a prophet in there," answered the peasant.

" Could he predict something for me ? " questioned the miller.

" Certainly : why not ? " answered the peasant; " but he can only prophesy four things, the fifth he keeps to himself."

The miller's curiosity was aroused. " Let him prophesy," he said.

Then the peasant tapped the raven on the head and it croaked, " Grr-grr."

" What's that he says ? " inquired the miller.

" First he says there is wine under the pillow."

" That means peep and see," said the miller, and he went and found the wine. " Now let him go on," the miller entreated.

The peasant made the raven croak again, and interpreted, " Secondly, there is roast meat in the coal scuttle," he says.

" That means peep and see," cried the miller. He looked and found the meat.

The peasant made the raven croak a third time, and said, " Thirdly, there is salad in the bed."

" That means peep and see," said the miller, and found the salad.

A fourth time the peasant tapped the raven, and said, " Fourthly, there is cake under the bed."

" Peep and see," cried the miller, and looked under the bed and found the cake.

The two now sat down to the loaded table, but the

miller's wife, in a desperate fright, reclined on the bed and partook of the dishes there. The miller wanted to hear the fifth thing the raven could tell, but the peasant said, "First let us eat the four things we have. The fifth is not so pleasant."

They ate to their hearts' content, and afterwards it was arranged how much the miller should pay for the prophecy. At last they settled on three hundred crowns.

Then the peasant tapped the raven once more on the head till it croaked loudly: "Outside, the devil is hiding in the linen press."

The miller said, "Then we must drive him away."

The miller's wife was obliged to give up the key, and the peasant opened the press, whereupon the priest came out and ran off as fast as his legs would carry him.

And the miller said, "I saw the black creature quite distinctly, and no mistake."

So the peasant started away next day in the twilight, with three hundred crowns in his pocket.

In time, the once poor little peasant built a pretty house, and the villagers remarked to each other, "He must have been in the country where it snows gold, and where people carry away bushels of it." So he was brought before the constable and ordered to explain where the riches came from.

He answered, "I sold my cow's skin for three hundred crowns."

When the villagers heard this they all ran home, killed their cows on the spot, took their skins and rushed off to the town to drive an equally advantageous bargain. The constable sent his own maid-servant on ahead in order that she might be first.

The tanner gave her not more that three crowns for a skin, and when the rest came he gave them less, saying, "What on earth am I to do with all these cow-hides?"

And now the villagers were enraged with poor Little Peasant, being sure he had cheated them. They were determined to be revenged, and had him up to answer for his trick before the constable. The innocent peasant was condemned to be put into a bottomless barrel and rolled into the river. So the peasant was led out and a clergyman sent for to read him the mass. The crowd withdrew, and left the peasant and the clergyman alone, and on the peasant looking closer, he recognised the priest who had been the guest of the miller's wife.

He said to him, " I was the means of your escaping from the press ; now help me to escape from the barrel."

Just then a shepherd passed, driving a flock of sheep, and it was a shepherd who had long cherished an ambition to be made constable.

" No, I'll never consent ! Never, never ! " shrieked the peasant with all his lungs.

The shepherd came up and said, " You'll never consent to what ? "

" They say if I sit in this barrel they will make me constable, and I say I will never consent," answered the peasant.

" Oh ! " exclaimed the shepherd, " if that's all one's got to do to become constable, I will gladly sit in the barrel."

" Well, then," said the peasant, " sit in it and you will be constable."

The shepherd complied readily, but no sooner had he crept into the barrel than the peasant slammed the lid. Then he took possession of the shepherd's flock and drove it away.

The priest went to the parishioners and said he had read the mass, and they all hurried to roll the barrel into the water.

As the barrel began to roll, the shepherd called out, " I will gladly be constable."

They replied, believing it to be the peasant, " We dare say ! But first you must explore down below," and they rolled the barrel into the water.

Afterwards all the villagers went home, and saw the peasant calmly driving a flock of sheep as if nothing had happened.

In the greatest amazement they cried, " Poor Little Peasant, where do you come from ? Have you got out of the water ? "

" Yes, of course," answered the peasant ; " I sank down, down, deeper and deeper till I reached the bottom, then I crept out, and there were lovely meadows beneath the water, with lambs grazing, so I brought a flock back with me."

"Are there any more to be had there?" asked all the villagers at once.

"Oh, yes," replied the peasant; "more than you can possibly want."

So the villagers set off in a band to get flocks for themselves, but the constable said, "I come first."

When they arrived at the water's edge, all over the blue sky were little fleecy clouds that people call flocks of sheep, and these were reflected in the water.

The villagers cried out, "Look! we can see them already."

The constable pushed forward. "I must go down first," he said, "and if all is well, I'll call you to follow."

He dived and made a great splash that sounded as if he had called, "Come on," and the whole lot dived in after him.

The village was now deserted, and poor Little Peasant became a wealthy man.

The Cobbler and The Tailor

ONCE a journeyman cobbler and journeyman tailor met on their wanderings. The tailor was a little, good-looking chap, always lively and full of jokes. When he saw the cobbler coming, and recognised his trade from the leather-cutter he carried, he burst into a mocking song—

> "Thread the needle,
> Draw the last,
> Daub it right and left with wax,
> Strike, strike as hard as you can."

The cobbler could not stand a joke, and made a grimace as if he had been drinking vinegar, threatening to take the tailor by the scruff of his neck and shake him.

The little chap began to laugh heartily, handed him his bottle, and said, " I didn't mean any harm. Take a good swig and swallow your anger."

The cobbler obeyed, and the thundercloud began to clear from his face. He handed back the bottle to the tailor saying, " It was thirst that made me touchy. Shall we wander further in company ? "

" I shall be delighted," said the tailor, " if you have a mind to visit a large town where there is sure to be work."

" Just what I should like," said the cobbler. " There is nothing going in a village, and in the country one is reduced to walking barefoot."

They therefore stepped out together. For a long time they did not get much to eat or drink, but when they came at last to a town they went round and called on the trades-men, and as the little tailor looked so fresh and gay, and had such pretty, rosy cheeks, everyone gave him some-thing, and the daughters of the master-tailor gave him a kiss to cheer him on his road.

When he joined the cobbler again he had a great deal more in his bundle, and the cross-grained cobbler made a sour face and said something about " the greater the rogue, the greater his luck."

The tailor, not in the least offended, laughed and divided all he had with his comrade.

They wandered on again and came to a huge forest, through which lay the road to a royal city. There were two paths ; one took two days and the other seven, but neither knew which was the shorter.

The two wanderers sat under an oak tree and consulted what they should do and for how many days they should supply themselves with bread. The cobbler said, " One must take thought for the morrow and look ahead. I shall take bread to last for seven days."

" What ! " exclaimed the tailor, " load oneself with bread for seven days, like a beast of burden ? I will rather trust God to feed me. The money in my pocket keeps as well in summer as in winter, but bread dries up in the heat and gets hard. What is there to prevent us finding the right way ? I shall buy bread for two days, but no more." So each bought their supply of bread and made their way into the forest.

It was still and quiet, like the inside of a church. Not a breath of wind stirred, no brook gurgled, or bird sang, and not a ray of sunlight penetrated the thick foliage.

The cobbler did not talk at all, for his weight of bread made his back ache, and perspiration poured from his sour gloomy visage.

The tailor, on the other hand, was merry, skipped about, whistled on a leaf, or sang a snatch of song, and thought, " It must please God in heaven to see me so happy."

Two days passed, and on the third the forest had not come to an end, but the tailor's bread had, and his spirits sank a little ; all the same he did not lose heart, but put faith in God and his good luck. On the night of the third day he lay down to sleep hungry, and woke up the next morning hungrier still. So it went on through the fourth day.

The cobbler sat on the stump of a tree and devoured his meal, while there was nothing for the tailor to do but to look on. If he implored the cobbler to bestow on him a morsel of bread, the cobbler laughed contemptuously. " You have always been so merry and gay, now see what it feels like not to be merry," he said. " The birds who sing in the morning are often snared before evening." In short, the cobbler had no compassion.

On the fifth morning the poor tailor could hardly stand

for exhaustion, and was almost too weak to speak. His cheeks were pale and his eyes red.

Then the cobbler said, " I will give you a piece of bread, but in return you must let me put out your right eye."

The unfortunate tailor, who wanted to live, saw no alternative but to consent to this arrangement. He cried once more with both eyes, and then the cobbler, who had a heart of stone, poked the right one out with a sharp knife.

The tailor remembered an old saying of his mother's, which he had heard her speak in the store-room after he had eaten good things, "Eat as much as you can, and suffer afterwards." When he had finished his dearly bought bread, he got on his legs again, forgot his trouble and comforted himself with the thought that he could still see with one eye. But on the sixth day the pangs of hunger were worse than ever, and at night he fell down under a tree, and the next morning could not rise for exhaustion, and he saw he was face to face with death.

The cobbler then said, " I will show mercy and give you more bread, if you will let me put out your other eye."

Then the tailor saw how frivolous his life had been, prayed to God for forgiveness, and said, "Do with me what you will, but remember that our Father in heaven judges all, and that an hour will come when you will have to expiate your evil doing, which I have not deserved at your hands. In brighter days I shared my all with you. My trade requires eyesight. With no eyes I shall not be able to stitch and must go a-begging. I pray you, therefore, when you have blinded me, not to leave me here alone to perish."

The cobbler had no pity in his heart. He took the knife and gouged out his companion's left eye, then he gave him a slice of bread, handed him a stick, and led him after him.

When the sun went down they came out of the forest into a field on which a gallows stood. The cobbler led the blind tailor up to it, left him there, and went his way.

The unfortunate little man, from weariness, pain, and hunger, fell asleep and slept the whole night. At dawn he awoke and did not know where he was. Two poor sinners hung on the gallows, and on the head of each was perched a carrion-crow. Then one of them began to speak.

"Brother, are you awake?" he asked.

"Yes, I am awake," answered the second.

"Then I will tell you something," the first spoke again. "The dew which this night had fallen on the gallows restores the sight if the eyes are washed with it. How many blind people, if they knew it, would get back their sight!"

Directly the tailor heard this he shook his handkerchief, rubbed it in the grass, and when it was soaked with dew, washed his empty sockets. And what the man on the gallows had said came true, for a pair of new, strong eyeballs grew at once in his sockets. The tailor saw the sun rise behind the mountains; before him in the valley lay the great royal city, with its towers and spires and gorgeous cupolas, its golden fanes flashing in the morning sunlight. He could distinguish every leaf on the trees, and saw all the birds that flew past and the gnats that danced in the air. He whipped a needle out of his pocket, and as he could thread it as easily as ever, his heart bounded with joy. He threw himself on his knees and thanked God for His mercies, and he did not forget to remember in his prayers the poor creatures hanging on the gallows. Then he put his bundle on his back, forgot his late sufferings and misery, and went onwards, whistling and singing.

The first thing he met was a brown foal frisking about in the fields. He caught it by the mane and would have jumped on its back and ridden to the town, but the foal begged to be allowed its freedom. "I am too young," it said, "and even a light tailor like you might break my back. Let me go, and one day I may be able to reward you."

"Run off, then," said the tailor, "I see you are a Spring-hill-Jack." He gave it a slash of the whip, and in its joy the foal threw up its hind legs and plunged over hedges and ditches away into the next field.

The little tailor had eaten nothing since the day before. "The sun," he said, "fills my eyes, but there's no bread in my mouth. The first thing I meet that is at all eatable I must kill." And then he saw a stork coming towards him over the meadow. "Stop!" he cried, and seized it by the leg. "I don't know whether you are good to eat, but my hunger gives me no choice. I must kill and roast you!"

"Don't do it, please," besought the stork. "I am a

sacred bird and I have never done any mischief, but, on the contrary, I am of great benefit to man. Give me my life and I will repay you one day."

"Run along, then, cousin longshanks," said the tailor, and the stork rose, letting its long legs hang down, and flew away.

"What is to be done?" said the tailor to himself. "My hunger becomes greater and my stomach emptier, and every opportunity that comes in my way I let slide." Just at that moment he saw some ducks swimming on a pond. "They have appeared as if by magic," he thought, and caught one. But just as he was going to wring its neck the old duck in the reeds set up a piteous shriek, waddled hastily forward with parted beak, and imported him to spare the life of her child.

"Think," she said, "of how your mother would have felt if you had been stolen from her and eaten!"

"Don't cry," said the good-natured tailor, "you shall keep your children," and he put the prisoner back in the water. He turned round and found himself standing in front of a half-hollow tree, in and out of which bees were flying. "Here I find the reward of my kindness," he said. "Honey will feed me."

But the queen bee came out, threatening him, and said, "If you interfere with my people and disturb the hive our stings will drive into your skin like ten thousand red-hot needles! Let us alone and go your way, and another time we will be of service to you."

The little tailor saw that here, too, three was no succour. "Three empty dishes and nothing on the fourth," he said is hardly a satisfying meal." So he dragged himself with his empty stomach into the great city, where he arrived at noon. He entered a tavern and sat down to table, ate, and was filled. Directly he was satisfied he exclaimed, "Now I will work!"

He went round the town searching for a good situation, and this was not hard to find, for he was a master of his trade and knew it in all its branches. He soon made a reputation, and was quite the fashion, everyone wanting his coat to be cut by the little tailor. Every day his fame increased. "And though I cannot become more perfect in my art,"

he thought, " my prospects grow brighter daily." At last
the king appointed him Court tailor.

But how strangely are things arranged in this life !
On the very same day his former comrade was made Court
cobbler. When the cobbler saw the tailor with two sound
eyes in his head his conscience pricked him. " Before he
is revenged on me," he thought, " I must try and dig him
a grave." But he who would dig a grave for others often
tumbles into it himself. In the evening, at dusk, the cobbler
slunk to the king and said, " Your Majesty, the tailor is a
bold fellow, and has the presumption to say he will find
and restore the golden crown that was lost centuries ago."

" I am glad to hear it," said the king, and the next
morning he summoned the tailor and commanded him to
produce the crown instantly or leave the town for ever.

" Indeed," thought the tailor, " only a rogue can give
more than he's got. Besides, if the pig-headed king
desires what it is impossible for any man to procure, I
will leave the city of my own accord, and not wait till the
morning." So he took his bundle, but as he passed out
of the gates he was sorry to think he was turning his back
on the city where he had been so happy and prosperous.

He then came to the pond where he had made acquaintance with the ducks. The old duck to whom he had
spared her duckling was seated on the bank preening
her feathers. She recognised him at once and asked why
he hung his head.

" You won't wonder," he said, " when I tell you what
has befallen me," and he related his story.

" If that's all," said the old duck, " I can give you advice.
The crown is in the water, and lies on the ground at the
bottom. I'll fetch it for you. Spread your pocket-hand-
kerchief out on the bank." She dived under with her
twelve ducklings, and after five minutes they all came
above the water with the crown in their midst. They
swam with it to the land, and laid the crown on the tailor's
handkerchief. You have no idea what a magnificent
crown it was. It flashed in the sun like a hundred carbuncles.. The tailor tied the crown up in his handkerchief
and carried it to the king, who was charmed to get it and
put a chain of gold round the tailor's neck.

When the cobbler saw that his scheme had failed he concocted another. He went to the king and said, "Your Majesty, the tailor has become so conceited that he imagines he can make a model in wax of the whole castle and everything inside and outside of it."

The king ordered the tailor to come into his presence, and told him to make a model in wax of the castle and everything inside and outside of it, and it must be exact down to the minutest detail. If so much as a single nail on the wall was left out he would be put in an underground dungeon for the rest of his life.

The tailor thought, "This is worse and worse. No human being can do it," and he threw his bundle over his shoulder and wandered outside the city.

As he came near the hollow tree the bees came flying out, and the queen bee inquired if he had a stiff neck, as he was holding his head crooked.

"I have something on my mind," he said, and told them what it was.

The bees began to buzz and hum together, and then the queen bee said, "Go home and come again to-morrow at this time, bringing with you a large cloth, and all will be well."

He turned homewards, while the bees swarmed on the castle and through the open windows, creeping into every corner and cranny, taking stock of and examining every detail. Then they flew back to their hive and made a model castle in wax with such rapidity that it seemed to grow like a mushroom. By the evening it was quite ready, and when the tailor came next morning the beautiful model was standing there complete, not a nail on the wall or a tile on the roof missing, the whole exquisitely delicate, and pure white and smelling of honey. The tailor packed it very carefully in his cloth and took it to the king, who could not admire it enough. It was placed in the large banqueting hall, and the tailor was presented in reward with a stone house to live in.

The cobbler, however, was not to be done and went a third time to the king, saying, "Your Majesty, the tailor has heard that no water can be made to spring up in the castle courtyard, and he has undertaken to produce a fountain that shall spring as high as a man and be clear as crystal."

So the king sent for the tailor and said, " I insist on your causing to spring up in my courtyard a jet of water such as you have described by this time to-morrow. If you can't do it my executioner shall reduce your height by a head."

The poor tailor, without reflection, ran out of the city gates half-distracted, as this time it was a case of life or death. Great tears rolled down his cheeks.

In this sorrowful plight he met the foal bounding along, now grown into a pretty brown horse. " The hour has come," said the horse, " in which I can repay you for letting me go that day. I know what is the matter, and you shall soon be helped out of your trouble. Get on my back. I could now carry two riders of your size."

The tailor recovered his spirits ; he sprang on the horse's back, and was soon galloping at full speed to the town. Straight into the courtyard his steed carried him, and after riding round and round at a dizzy pace there was a sudden explosion and the horse fell on its knees. On the spot the earth cracked and up sprang a jet of water higher than man and horse ; the water was as clear as crystal and the sunbeams danced on it. The king saw it in wonder and admiration, and, rushing to the little tailor, embraced him in the sight of everybody.

But even this happiness did not last long. The king had plenty of daughters, but no son. So the wicked cobbler went to the king a fourth time and said, " Majesty, the tailor has not ceased to boast. He says now he can bring your Majesty a son through the air."

The king sent for the tailor and said to him, " If you can get me a son in nine days you shall have my eldest daughter to be your wife."

" A great reward undoubtedly," thought the tailor, " but the fruit grows too high. If I climb to reach it the bough will certainly snap." He went home and sat with crossed legs by his work-table wondering what he should do. " It's no good," he sighed at last, " I must go away. Here I shall never be left in peace."

He took his bundle and hurried out of the city. When

he reached the meadows he beheld his old friend the stork, who stood like a sage contemplating a frog, which, after close examination, he finally swallowed.

Then the stork advanced and greeted him. " I see," he said, " that you have your knapsack on your back. Why do you leave the city ? "

The tailor told him of the king's behest and of the impossibility of performing it.

" Don't let your hair turn grey over that," said the stork, " I will help you out of your difficulty. For a long time I have been accustomed to bring babies in arms into the town, so I can easily fetch a little prince out of the well. Go home and keep calm. In nine days from now go to the castle and I will meet you there."

The little tailor went home, and at the appointed time turned up at the castle.

Soon afterwards the stork flew there and tapped at the window.

The tailor opened it ; Cousin Longshanks came in cautiously, and walked gravely and majestically over the marble floor. He had a child in his beak as beautiful as an angel, and it held out its tiny arms to the queen. The stork laid it in her lap, and she hugged it and kissed it rapturously, and was beside herself for joy. The stork before departing took his satchel off his shoulder and left it with the queen. It contained dates and all kinds of sweetmeats which were to be divided among the younger princesses. The eldest was given none, because she was to have the jolly little tailor for her husband.

He said, " My mother's words have come true. She always said trust in God and a merry heart would carry a man through all and bring him great happiness in the end."

The cobbler had to make the shoes in which the tailor danced at his wedding, and afterwards he was ordered out of the city. He took the path that led to the gallows. Worn out with rage, baffled malice, and the heat of the day, he threw himself down to rest. As he shut his eyes two crows swooped down with a scream from the gallows and picked out his eyes. He rushed into the forest, mad with pain, and must have perished there, for he was never seen or heard of again.

K

Drudge-of-all-work

THERE was once a king who had a wife with golden hair. She was so lovely that there was not her equal on earth. One day she fell ill and, feeling sure she would die, she called her husband and said, " If you marry again after I am dead, do not choose anyone as your wife who is not as fair as I am, and who has not golden hair like mine. You must promise me this." After the king had promised she closed her eyes and died.

For a long time the king was inconsolable and would not hear of choosing another wife.

At last his advisers said, " There is no help for it. The king must marry again ; we cannot do without a queen."

Ambassadors were now despatched all over the world to look for a bride whose beauty should rival that of the late queen. They could not find anyone who approached her, and even if they had, she would not have had the same golden hair. So the ambassadors returned, abandoning the quest as hopeless.

The king had a daughter who grew up as beautiful as her dead mother, and who had golden hair like hers. The king looked at her one day and was struck by her extraordinary likeness in every respect to his dead wife. He said to his advisers, " I will marry my daughter, because she is the living image of my dead wife, and no one else in the world resembles her."

The advisers were horrified, and reminded him that God forbade a man to marry his daughter, and that if he committed such a sin no good would come to the kingdom. The daughter, too, was alarmed when she heard of her father's resolve, and tried to turn him from it. She said to him, " Before I can comply with your wish I must have three dresses, one gold like the sun, another silver like the moon, and a third shining like the stars; besides, I must have a cloak made of a thousand skins put together, and every animal in your kingdom shall contribute to this fur garment," As she said this she thought, "It is quite impossible that he can ever procure these, and my suggestions will deter him from his purpose."

The king, however, issued an order to the most skilful spinning women in his realm to set to work to spin the dresses, one gold like the sun, another silver like the moon, and the third shining like the stars; and the king's huntsmen were commissioned to catch every animal in the kingdom, to take a bit of the skin of each kind and construct the patch-work cloak of a thousand skins. At length, when all was finished, the king had the cloak spread before him and said, "To-morrow is the day fixed for the wedding."

The princess, seeing there was no hope of changing the king's purpose, determined to fly. In the night, when everyone was asleep, she got up and selected from among her jewels and valuables three things—a gold ring, a gold spinning-wheel, and a gold hare-skin. The dresses like the sun, moon, and stars, she folded up and laid in a nutshell. She put on the cloak of animal skins and stained her face and hands with walnut juice. Then she commended herself to God and set out.

She walked on and on the whole night, till she came to a large wood, and as she was worn out she sat down in a hollow tree and fell asleep. The sun rose, and still she slept and slept, far into the day.

Then it happened that the king to whom the wood belonged came to hunt in it. When his hounds came to the tree they jumped round it and barked.

The king said to the huntsmen, "Look and see what wild deer is hidden there."

The huntsmen obeyed, and when they came back said, "There is a marvellous animal in the hollow trunk, the like of which we have never seen before. It has a skin composed of a thousand kinds of fur, and it is lying asleep."

The king said, "Catch it alive, bind it to the waggon, and take it home."

When the huntsmen caught hold of the girl she awoke

in terror, and cried out, " I am a poor child, deserted by my father and mother ; have compassion upon me and treat me kindly."

They said, " Drudge-of-all-work, you'll do for the scullery, and can pick up the ashes."

So they bound her to the waggon, took her home to the royal castle, and showed her a cupboard under the stairs where there was no daylight, saying, " There, little wild animal, you may dwell, and sleep if you like." Then they sent her to the kitchen, where she had to hew wood, draw water, clean grates, sift the ashes, wash the vegetables, disembowel the game, and do all the dirty work and odd jobs.

Thus poor Drudge-of-all-work lived a long time in great wretchedness. Alas, poor princess, what a fate !

One day there was a great feast in the castle, and she said to the cook, " May I go upstairs and look on for a little ? I will hide behind the door."

The cook answered, " Yes, I give you leave ; but remember, in half an hour you must be back again to sift the ashes." So the princess took her little oil lamp and went into her cupboard, where she laid aside her fur covering and washed the stain off her hands and face, so that her beauty shone forth in all its radiance. Then she opened the nutshell and drew out the robe that shone like the sun. In it she went upstairs to the party, and every-one drew aside to let her pass, for no one recognised her, and all thought she was some strange princess.

The king came forward, kissed her hand, and danced with her, thinking he had never before set eyes on so beautiful a creature.

When the dance was over, she curtsied ; and when the king looked round she had vanished, no one knew where. The guards in front of the castle were called and questioned, but not one of them had seen her pass. She had run back to her cupboard, hastily taken off her dress, made her hands and face sooty, wrapped herself in the fur mantle again, and was once more Drudge-of-all-work.

When she went back to her work in the kitchen the cook said, " Leave the cinders till to-morrow and make the king's soup for me, while I go up and look on for a bit too ; but.

whatever you do, don't let a hair get into the soup, or in future I shall give you no more scraps to eat."

The cook departed and Drudge-of-all-work made the king's soup. It was a bread soup, and she took great pains with it. When it was ready she went to her cupboard, fetched her gold ring and laid it in the dish in which the soup was to be served.

After the dance was over the king ordered his soup to be brought, tasted it, and said it was so good, that he never remembered to have tasted better. As he came to the bottom of the bowl he saw the golden ring and could not conceive how it had come there. He ordered the cook to be brought into his presence.

The cook was in a great fright at this summons and said to Drudge-of-all-work, " I expect you have let a hair fall into the soup. If you have, I'll give you a hiding."

" Who made the soup ? " asked the king when the cook stood before him.

" I made it," replied the cook.

The king, however, said, " That is not true ; it was made in a different way and was much better than usual."

Then the cook said, " I must confess that it was not I, but the little ragamuffin who made the soup."

" Send her to me, then," commanded the king.

When Drudge-of-all-work appeared the king asked, " Who are you ? "

She replied, " I am a poor orphaned child, with neither father nor mother."

" What are you doing in the castle ? " he questioned again.

" Nothing. I am only good for having boots thrown at my head," she answered humbly.

" Where did you get the ring that was in my soup ? "

" The ring ? What ring ? I know nothing about it."

The king, finding he could get nothing out of her, sent her back to the kitchen.

Not long afterwards there was another feast in the castle, and Drudge-of-all-work asked permission of the cook, as before, to go up and watch the merry-making.

The cook said, " Yes, you can go, but come back in half an hour and make the bread soup the king likes so much."

The princess ran off to her cupboard, washed herself quickly, and shook out the robe that was silver like the moon, arrayed herself in it and went upstairs to the ballroom. The king advanced to receive her, expressed his delight at meeting the fair princess again, and they danced together. But immediately the dance was over she vanished so quickly that the king did not see which direction she fled in. She popped into her cupboard, converted herself into a towzled-headed little ragamuffin again, and went into the kitchen to cook the bread soup. While the cook was upstairs she fetched her little gold spinning-wheel and placed it in the dish in which the soup was to be served. The soup was taken up to the king, who ate it with relish, saying it was the best he had ever tasted.

Again the cook was sent for, and she was obliged to confess, as before, that not she but Drudge-of-all-work had made the soup.

Once more Drudge-of-all-work was summoned, but she would say nothing except that boots were thrown at her head, and that she knew nothing about gold spinning-wheels.

A third time the king gave a banquet in his castle and things happened as they had done on the two previous occasions.

The cook said, " You certainly must be a witch, ragamuffin, otherwise how is it the soup tastes so much better to the king when you make it ? "

But the girl begged so hard to be allowed to go up and watch the dancing that the cook said she might. This time she put on the dress that shone like the stars. She entered the hall, and the king danced with her and thought she looked lovelier than ever. While they were dancing, the king, unremarked, slipped a ring on to his partner's finger and gave orders for the dance to be prolonged. When at last the dance was over he tried to hold her fast by both hands, but she snatched them away and hurried off so quickly through the crowd that she seemed to vanish before his very eyes. As fast as she could, she ran into her cupboard beneath the stairs, but because she had been absent over half an hour she had not time to take off the starry dress, but threw her fur cloak over it, and in her haste she forgot to make herself quite sooty, and one finger remained white.

Drudge-of-all-work now ran into the kitchen, made the king's bread soup, and when the cook was away looking on at the dance she laid the golden hare-skin in the tureen.

The king when he found it ordered Drudge-of-all-work to be brought to him. At once he detected her white finger and the ring he had put on it during the dance. He caught hold of her hand and held it tight, and when she tried to disengage herself her fur mantle opened a little in front and he saw the star robe shining between the folds. Then her golden hair came to view, and it was impossible for her to conceal herself any longer. When she had wiped the cinders and soot from her face she looked more beautiful than any earthly being.

The king said, " Now I will make you my bride, and we will never part again." So they were married and lived happily together till the end of their days.

The Earth Mannikin

A WEALTHY king had three daughters who took exercise every day in the castle garden, where were many tall and beautiful trees. If you plucked an apple off one of these and bit it you at once sank a hundred feet into the earth. So people were forbidden to pick the fruit. In the autumn the apples on this particular tree became as red as blood. Every day the three daughters stood under the branches to see if the wind had blown down any of the fruit, but none fell, although some of the twigs touched the earth, the tree was so laden.

The youngest of the three sisters was seized with a great longing to taste one of the apples, and said to the others, "Our father loves us far too well to let us be punished for picking an apple; he has only made the rule for strangers, I am sure." The child then picked a big red apple, and, after biting it, cried, "Just taste, dear sisters. It is the sweetest, juiciest apple you can imagine. Never in my life have I tasted anything so delicious." Then both the other princesses bit the apple, and instantly they all sank into the earth, and not a single hair of them was to be seen.

At midday the king sent for them, but they were nowhere to be found, though castle and garden were ransacked. Then the king ordered the whole country to be searched, and promised that whoever found his daughters should be given the hand of one in marriage. Quite a crowd of young people started off to look—for everyone was fond of the three maidens, they were so pretty and frank and friendly in their manners. Among the search party were three young huntsmen who, after they had journeyed for eight days, arrived at a great castle in which there were spacious apartments. In one of the rooms a table was covered with tempting dishes, so hot that they steamed, but not a soul was to be seen in the whole castle. They waited half a day and the food kept hot and continued to steam, until at last their hunger became so intense that they could not resist satisfying it. Then they decided to remain in the castle, and arranged that two should stop at home while the other went out to search for the three lost daughters. The lot fell to the eldest. But the next day the two youngest went out to search, and the eldest was obliged to stay in. At midday there came a tiny little man to fetch bread, and the huntsman cut him a round, but directly he handed it to the little man he dropped it, and then demanded that it should be picked up. The huntsman stooped to obey, and the little man took his stick and, holding him by the hair, administered three heavy blows. The next time he was left at home he fared no better. When the other two came back they said to the eldest :

" How have you got on ? "

" Why, badly," was the answer ; and he related what had happened.

The third day the youngest stayed at home, and the tiny little man came and asked for bread, and when he was given a slice dropped it, and ordered that it should be picked up as before.

Then the youngest brother said to the little man, " If you can't take the trouble to do it yourself you are not worth your daily bread."

The little fellow grew furious and insisted that he should do it for him ; but the other still refused, and took hold of the little man's coat, thrashed him, and threatened to turn him out.

" Leave go, leave go," he screamed, " and I'll show you the place where the princesses are hidden."

When the youth heard this he left off drubbing the little man, who informed him that he was an earth mannikin, and if he would accompany him he would show him where the three lost princesses were. He then showed him a well in which the water was dried up, and said :

" Your companions do not mean to act honestly, so if you would rescue the three maidens you must go alone. The two others would, of course, like to find the three daughters, but they have not the courage for the enterprise. You must take a great basket and sit in it with a dagger and a bell, and let yourself down. Underneath you will find three rooms ; in each will be a princess guarded by a dragon with several heads. You must cut off the heads."

When he had given these instructions the earth mannikin vanished.

At evening, when the two others returned, they asked how their brother had fared at home all alone.

He said, " Oh, pretty well. I was eating my lunch at noon when a strange little fellow came and begged for a slice of bread, and on my giving it to him he let it fall and told me to pick it up. I didn't see it, and on his becoming insolent I thrashed him, and he revealed to me where the princesses were hidden."

The two were dreadfully annoyed at this and grew green and yellow from jealousy.

The next morning, however, they all three cast lots at the empty well as to which should sit in the basket. The lot fell to the eldest, who seated himself and took the bell. He said, " If I ring you two must draw me up quickly." He was lowered and rang immediately, so they drew him up. The next lot fell to the youngest. He was lowered, and when he got out of the basket he took his dagger and stood at the door of the first room listening. He heard the dragon snore distinctly, broke open the door, and saw one of the princesses sitting surrounded by nine dragons' heads. He raised his dagger and cut off the nine heads. The princess sprang up, threw her arms round his neck and kissed him rapturously. Then he went on to the next princess, and found her in the company of a dragon with seven heads. These he cut off, and came to the third princess, whose dragon had four heads, which he dispatched likewise. Then all three of the king's daughters surrounded and hugged and thanked him for their deliverance. He rang the bell so loudly that it was heard above and he put the princesses one after the other in the basket and they were all three drawn up. Then the words that the earth mannikin had spoken about his brothers not meaning to act honestly occurred to him. So he took a huge stone, and laid it in the basket. It was drawn about half-way up, then the wicked brothers cut the rope, and the basket and the stone fell heavily to the ground.

The brothers, thinking that he was in it, ran off with the princesses, making them promise to tell the king they had delivered them.

Then the king offered the young men the hands of his daughters in marriage.

Meanwhile the youngest huntsman wandered about underground in the three chambers, thinking he must die, when suddenly he saw a flute hanging on the wall. " What is the good of hanging in this sad place, flute ? " he said. " Here you cannot tune up." Then he looked at the dragons' heads. " You cannot help me, either," he said. He walked up and down so many times that the ground became smooth and slippery. It then struck him that he might amuse himself by taking the flute from the wall and blowing a tune on it. All at once up rose earth mannikins, one for every note he played, till the room was choke-full of mannikins.

They all asked him what he wished, and he said he wanted to go up on the earth again and see daylight. So each caught hold of a hair of his head and lifted him up on the earth.

He made at once for the king's castle, where the marriage festivities of one of the daughters were already being celebrated.

The three daughters, on seeing him, became quite faint.

The king was angry, thinking he had done his children some harm, and ordered him to prison.

But when the princesses came to themselves they besought that he might be set at liberty.

The king asked why they wanted him set free, and they said they could not tell him, but if he went and listened at the stove-pipe he would hear all. He went, and the result was that the two wicked brothers were sent to the gallows, and the good one was given the youngest princess.

At her wedding she wore a pair of glass slippers, which were cracked because she stepped on a stone on her way from the church.

The Six Swans

A KING once hunted a wild stag so eagerly that none of his followers could keep up with him. As evening drew on, he paused and looked round, and saw that he had lost the track completely. Everywhere he looked for a way out, but none was to be found. Then he saw an old woman with a palsied head coming towards him. She was a witch, but he addressed her, and said, "My good woman, can you show me the way out of the wood?"

"Yes, sir king," she answered, I can, but on one condition, which if you do not fulfil you must stay in the wood and die of hunger."

"What is the condition?" asked the king.

"I have a daughter," said the old woman, "who is as pretty a girl as is to be seen anywhere in the world, and is worthy to be your queen. Marry her and I will show you the path out of the wood."

The king was so alarmed at his position that he at once consented, and the old woman led him to her house, where her daughter was sitting by the fire. The girl received the king as if she had been expecting him, and although he could not but admit that she was beautiful, he did not take to her, and was filled with secret horror at the sight of her. When he had placed the girl on his saddle the old woman showed him the way out of the forest. He reached his royal castle safely and the marriage was solemnised.

Now the king had been married before, and had had seven children by his first wife, six boys and one girl, whom he loved better than anything else in the world. Because he was afraid the stepmother might not treat the children well and would do them some injury, he had them shut up in a solitary castle in the middle of a wood. It lay so far from the beaten track that it was difficult to find, and he himself could not have found the way had not a wise woman given him a ball of yarn of such a marvellous quality that when he threw it in front of him it unwound itself and showed the direction.

The king went so often to his dear children that the new queen noticed how often he was absent, and was curious to know where he went and what he did all alone in the wood. She bribed the servants, and they at last betrayed the secret, and told her of the ball which alone could show the way. After that she could not rest till she had discovered where the king kept the ball. Then she made several little white silk shirts, and as she had learnt magic arts from her mother, she sewed magic into the shirts with every stitch.

So once, when the king had gone hunting, she took the little shirts and went into the wood, and the ball of yarn showed her the path. The children, hearing someone coming in the distance, thought it was their father, and rushed to meet him full of joy. Thereupon the queen threw a shirt over each, and immediately the children were turned into swans and flew away out of the wood.

The queen went home pleased with her day's work, thinking she had got rid of her stepchildren, but the little girl had not run out with the others to meet her, and the queen did not know of her existence.

The next day the king went to see his children and found only the girl. "Where are your brothers?" he inquired.

"Ah! dear father," she answered, "they have gone away and left me alone." She related how she had looked out of her window and seen them all changed into swans, and she showed the king the feathers they had dropped in the yard as they flew away.

The king grieved, but he had no suspicion that the queen had been guilty of the crime, and, because he feared something might happen to his daughter too, he proposed to take her home.

But the child was frightened of her stepmother, and begged to be allowed to stay one more night in the woodland castle. The poor child thought to herself, "I am no use to anyone without my brothers, I will go and look for them." When night came on she escaped and fled into the wood.

The whole night, the next day, and the next, she walked on and on till for very weariness she could go no further. Then she saw a forester's hut, went up the steps, and found a room with six little beds in it. She dare not trust herself to lie down on one of the beds, so she crept underneath, intending to pass the night on the hard floor. Just as the sun was going down, however, she heard a rustling and saw that six swans had flown in at the window. They sat on the floor, blew on each other, and blew all their feathers off, and then stripped off their swan-skin like a shirt. When the girl saw they were her brothers she was overjoyed and crept out from under the bed.

They were not less pleased at seeing their little sister again, but their joy was of short duration. "This is no place for you to stay in," they said to her, "it is a refuge for robbers, and when they come and find you they will murder you."

"Couldn't you protect me?" asked the little sister.

"No," they answered, "because we may only lay aside our swan-plumage for a quarter of an hour every evening; then we may assume human form, but we are changed back again into swans afterwards."

The sister cried, and said, "Couldn't you be released from the spell?"

"Alas, no!" they answered, "the conditions are too severe. You would have to go six years without speaking or laughing, and in that time would have to make us six shirts out of primroses. If one single word passed your lips all the labour would be thrown away."

No sooner had the brothers told her these conditions than the quarter of an hour was up, and in the shape of swans they flew out of the window again.

The girl, however, resolved to free her brothers, even if it cost her her life. She left the hut, went into the wood, climbed a tree, and passed the night there. The next morning she went out and gathered primroses, and began to sew. There was no one to speak to, and she had no inclination to laugh, or to do anything but sit at her work.

She had been thus employed for a long time, when it happened that the king of the country came with his huntsmen to the tree on which the maiden sat. They called out, "Who are you?" But she made no reply. "Come down here to us," they said, "we won't hurt you." In response she only shook her head. When they continued to ply her with questions she threw down her gold necklace, hoping that would satisfy them. Still they would not go away, so she took off her sash and threw that down, and then her garters, and by degrees every article of clothing she could spare, till she was left with nothing but her undergarments.

The huntsmen were not going to be put off with her clothes; they climbed up the tree, carried her down, and led her to the king.

The king asked, "Who are you, and what are you doing up in the tree?" But she did not answer. He asked the question in every language he knew, and she remained as dumb as a fish. But because of her beauty the king's heart was touched, and he fell greatly in love with her. He threw his cloak over her, put her on his horse, and brought her to his castle. Here she was arrayed in rich garments, and she was as radiant in her beauty as the summer day, yet no word passed her lips. She sat by the king's side at table, and her modest bearing pleased him so much that he exclaimed, "This is the maiden I wish to wed, and no other in the world," and a few days later he married her.

The king, unfortunately, had a wicked mother, who was not satisfied with her son's choice, and who spoke evil of the young queen. "Who knows what the hussy may be?" she said. "A dumb creature is not a fit person to be queen."

In about a year the queen bore her first child. The old woman took it away from her, and while she was asleep daubed the young mother's mouth with blood. Then she went to the king and accused his wife of being a cannibal. The king would not believe it, and said he would not have anything done to her. She sat quietly at her work, busily hemming the shirts and thinking of nothing else.

The next time she brought a pretty boy into the world, and the wicked mother-in-law practised the same decep-

tion. And again the king refused to believe the story. He
said, "She is so pious, kind, and gentle, it is impossible
that she could do such a thing. If she could speak and
defend herself her innocence would be as clear as daylight."

But when a third time the new-born babe was stolen by
the old hag, and the queen was charged with cannibalism,
yet did not make any defence, the king could not help himself, and was obliged to hand her over to the judges, who
condemned her to be burnt to death.

When the day came on which the sentence was to be
carried out, the last day of the six years was up, the period
in which she had promised never to speak or to laugh, and
she had freed her dear brothers from the spell. The six
shirts were all finished, except that one still wanted a sleeve.

As she was led to the scaffold the queen took the shirts
on her arm. As she stood there and the faggots round her
were just going to be set alight she saw six swans flying
through the air. Now she knew that her release was coming,
and her heart beat fast with joy. The swans descended and
came quite near, so that she could throw the shirts over
them, and directly they came in contact witth the shirts the
swan-skins fell off, and her brothers stood in the flesh before
her, fresh and strong and handsome; only the youngest
had instead of a left arm a swan's wing. They embraced
and kissed each other, and then the queen went to the king
and said:

"Dearest husband, now I may speak and tell you I am
innocent and that I have been falsely accused." And she
related the whole story of the old woman's deceit, and how
her three children had been taken away and hidden.

To the great delight of the king the children were now
produced, and the wicked stepmother was condemned to
death, and was burnt to ashes on the scaffold. The king
and queen with her six brothers lived happily ever after.

The Magic Wallet, Hat and Horn

ONCE upon a time there were three brothers who became poorer and poorer, till at last they had nothing wherewith to satisfy their hunger. Then they said to one another, "Things cannot go on thus. We had better go out into the world and try our luck."

They started, and had gone a good way over hill and dale, but still had not met with any luck. Then they came to a huge wood, in the middle of which was a mound, and as they came nearer it proved to be full of silver. The eldest said, "Now I have found all the happiness I can desire," and he filled his pockets and took as much silver as he could carry away. He went home, but the other two said, "We want something more than mere silver to make us happy," and, instead of helping themselves to the metal, they pushed forwards.

After tramping for about two days they came to a mound of gold. The second brother stood still, reflected, and was undecided. "What shall I do?" he said. "Shall I take gold enough to last me all my life, or shall I go on?" At last he decided to fill his pockets with as much gold as they would hold, bade his brother farewell, and went home.

The third, however, said, "Silver and gold are not for me. I will seek my happiness elsewhere. Perhaps something better is in store. Who knows?"

He tramped on, and after three days came to a wood that was so big that there seemed no end to it, and, as he had nothing to eat or drink, he thought he would perish of hunger. Then he climbed up a high tree to see where the wood ended, but saw nothing but the tops of trees. He dropped off the tree again, and was so tormented with the pangs of hunger that he could not help saying aloud, "If only I had something to satisfy my appetite!" To

L

his astonishment, there, at the foot of the tree, was a table spread with hot delicacies, the steam from which rose in his face. "My wish fulfilled in the nick of time," he exclaimed, and, without troubling as to where the food had come from, or who had cooked it, he sat down and ate heartily till his hunger was appeased. When he had finished he said to himself, "It would be a pity to leave this dainty table-cloth to spoil here in the wood," so he folded it up neatly and put it in his pocket.

He walked on, and in the evening, when he became hungry again, resolved to put the little cloth to the test. Laying it out, he said, "How I wish you would spread yourself with good things again!" Scarcely had the wish passed his lips than there stood before him more dishes than he could count, filled to overflowing with delicious viands.

"Now I know," he said, "in what kitchen my food is cooked. This cloth is worth more than mountains of silver and gold." For he saw the little cloth had magic properties, and was a spread-of-itself table-cloth. However, he was not inclined to sit down with this priceless possession and stay always in the same place. He wanted to see the world and find happiness.

One evening he came into a very dreary, lonely wood, where he met a coal-black charcoal burner, who was burning coals and putting potatoes on to roast for his supper. "Good evening, blackamoor," said he. "How do you get along in this solitude?"

"One day is just like another," answered the charcoal burner. "Every evening I dine off potatoes. If you like them, will you be my guest to-night?"

"Many thanks," replied the traveller. "I will not rob you of your food. You are not prepared for a guest. If you have no objection, allow me to entertain you." Thereupon he took his table-cloth out of his wallet and spread it on the ground.

"I don't know how you can manage to entertain me if you have nothing but that," said the charcoal burner; "and in the country round here there isn't a house where you can procure food."

"All the same I am going to provide a dinner, and as

good a one as you ever tasted," said the traveller. Then he
added, "Little table-cloth, spread yourself," and behold
roast and boiled joints stood before them, as hot as if they
had just been dished up from the kitchen.

The charcoal burner looked surprised, as well he might,
but did not need a second invitation. He sat down
and crammed huge pieces into his sooty mouth. When
he had eaten as much as he could, he smirked and said,
"This table-cloth has won my esteem and approval.
It would be invaluable to me in this lonely wood to be
able to get a meal like that for nothing. I will propose an
exchange. Over there hangs an old military wallet which,
though shabby and unsightly, has magic properties ; but,
as I am tired of it, I will exchange it for your table-cloth."

"First I must know what its magic properties are,"
replied the stranger.

"I will tell you with pleasure," said the charcoal
burner. "Every time you tap on the top with your
hand out comes a corporal with six men armed from tip
to toe, and whatever you command them to do will be at
once performed."

"It's all the same to me," said the traveller. "If it
can't be helped, I don't mind changing with you." So he
gave the charcoal burner his table-cloth, took the wallet
from the bough it was hanging on, and said farewell.

After he had gone a little way he thought he would put
the powers of his wallet to the test, and tapped it.
Directly the seven warriors appeared, and the corporal
said, "What does my lord and master require ? "

"March back at double quick time and ask the charcoal
burner to give back my little cloth."

They turned right about face, and at once executed
the commission. Then he told them to retire, and proceeded on his way, looking forward to a still luckier future.

At sunset he came across another charcoal burner, who
was cooking his supper over a fire. "Will you sup with
me ? " he asked. "Potatoes, with salt for a relish. If
so, sit down."

"No," answered the traveller. "This once you shall
be my guest." He laid his table-cloth on the ground,
and it was soon covered with tempting dishes.

They ate and drank together, and were very content with the good things. After the meal the charcoal burner said, " Over there lies an old battered hat which has miraculous properties. You have only to put it on your head and twirl it round, and field artillery will spring up twelve at a time and annihilate whoever comes in their way. The hat is no good to me, and I will gladly exchange it for your cloth."

" Very well," was the answer, and he took the hat, put it on, and left the cloth behind him. Before he had gone far he tapped the wallet, and his soldiers were sent to fetch the cloth. " One thing comes after another, and I feel as if there were yet more luck in store for me," he thought. He was not deceived, for after another day's walk he came to a third charcoal burner who, like the others, invited him to sit down to boiled potatoes. He, instead, entertained him, and they dined off the wonderful cloth, which so delighted the charcoal burner that he offered in exchange for it a horn which was endowed with magic. When you blew on it all walls crashed and towns and villages fell in ruins. He gave the charcoal burner the cloth in exchange for the horn, but sent his men to recover it, so that finally he was in possession of wallet, hat, and horn.

" Now," said he, " I am a made man, and it is time I went home and looked up my brothers." He went home, and found that his brothers had built a beautiful house out of their silver and gold, and were living in ease and luxury. But because he wore a ragged coat and a shabby hat, and had a disreputable wallet on his back, they would not own him as their brother.

" You who despised silver and gold and talked of finding something better ! We should have thought you would at least have come home a king, not a mere beggar ! " And they turned him out of the house.

In great wrath he tapped so long and so furiously on his wallet that a hundred and fifty men came out and fell into line. He commanded them to surround his brothers' house, and selected two to go in and lay about their bodies with switches till their skin was blistered and smarted unbearably. There arose a tremendous outcry ; people ran hither and thither, and wanted to render the besieged brothers assistance, but were powerless against the soldiers.

At last the king heard what was going on, and sent an officer with an armed force to drive the disturber of the public peace out of the town ; but the man with the wallet soon had another supply of men at hand, and repulsed the king's soldiers.

The king said, " This vagabond fellow shall be squashed yet," and sent a larger force, but it was equally powerless. More men came out of the wallet, and, to make short work of his opponents, he twirled his hat two or three times, and there was such a deadly firing that the king's men were completely routed and took flight.

" I will only make peace," he said, " on one condition, and that is, that the king gives me his daughter as my wife and allows me to rule the kingdom."

The king, when he knew this, told his daughter and said, " What else can I do ? For the sake of peace and to keep the crown on my head, you must consent to become his wife."

The wedding was therefore celebrated, but the princess was exceedingly annoyed at having to marry a vulgar man who wore a shabby hat and an old wallet on his back. She was anxious to be quit of him, and meditated day and night how she could bring it about. She wondered to herself whether the wallet had anything to do with his extraordinary powers. So one day she caressed and flattered him till she brought him to a very yielding mood ; then she said, " If only you would lay aside that old wallet ! It disfigures you so much that I am quite ashamed of you."

" Dear child," he answered, " this wallet is my most priceless possession. So long as I have it I fear nothing on earth," and he confided to her its miraculous powers.

Then she threw her arms round his neck, and pretended she wanted to kiss him, but, instead, unfastened the wallet from his shoulder and ran away with it. As soon as she was alone she tapped it, and ordered the warriors to take their former master prisoner and lead him out of the palace. They obeyed, and the false woman set a crowd on him as well to hunt him out of the country.

He would have been lost if he had not had the battered hat. Directly he could free his hands he twirled it on his head, and the artillery began to thunder and shoot everybody down, and the princess had to come and pray for mercy. Because she implored him to spare her and promised never to be so wicked again, he let himself be talked over, and granted her her freedom. She then became friendly and kind, and seemed to be so fond of him that at last she coaxed him into telling her the secret of the hat as well as that of the wallet. So soon as she knew it she waited till he had fallen asleep, and then took the hat away. She threw it into the street, and he, waking up, was so furious at her deceit that he took the horn, which he still had left, and blew on it with all his might. Walls, fortresses, towns, villages immediately fell in ruins, and the king and the princess were killed. And if he had chosen to go on blowing his horn he could have destroyed the whole kingdom and left no stone standing, but he preferred to make himself king, and no one resisted him any more.

The Three Magic Gifts

A LONG time ago, there lived a tailor who had three sons and one goat. As the goat had to feed them all with its milk, it was necessary that it should have good fodder and be taken out to the meadow to graze every day. The sons took it in turns to go with the goat. Once the eldest led it to the churchyard, where the best herbs grew, and let it graze and jump about there. In the evening, when it was time to come home, he asked, " Are you satisfied, goat ? "

The goat answered :

> " I am so full,
> Another leaf I could not eat,
> Bleat ! bleat ! "

" So come home," said the boy ; and he put a cord round his neck and led him away and tied him up in the stable.

" Did the goat have its right fodder, and enough ? " asked the tailor.

" Oh, yes," answered the son. " She is so full she couldn't eat another leaf."

The father, however, wanted to convince himself, so he went to the stable, stroked his pet, and asked, " Goat, are you full ? "

The goat replied :

> " How should I be full ?
> Grazing on the graves,
> With not a leaf to eat ?
> Bleat ! bleat ! "

" What do I hear ? " cried the tailor ; and he ran out and

said to the boy, "You wicked boy! you said the goat was full, and instead you have let her starve." And in his wrath he took the yard-measure, and with a shower of blows drove him out.

The next day it was the second son's turn to take the goat out. He sought a place in the garden hedge where there were some tasty herbs and weeds; the goat stripped the hedge, and when it was evening and time to go home, he asked, "Goat, are you full?"

The goat answered:

> "I am so full,
> Another leaf I could not eat,
> Bleat! bleat!"

"So come home then," said the boy. He led him away, and tied him up in the stable.

"Now then," asked the old tailor, "has the goat had its proper food?"

"Oh," answered the son, "she is so full she couldn't eat another leaf."

But the tailor wasn't satisfied, and he went into the stable and asked, "Goat, are you full?"

The goat replied:

> "How should I be full?
> Grazing on the graves,
> With not a leaf to eat?
> Bleat! bleat!"

"The wicked rascal," cried the tailor, "to let a good animal like this starve!" And with the yard-measure he struck his son and drove him off.

It was the third son's turn the next day, and to be quite sure the goat should have good food, he selected a beautiful shrub and let the goat eat the leaves. When evening came and it was time to go home, he asked, "Goat, are you full?"

The goat answered:

> "I am so full,
> Another leaf I could not eat.
> Bleat! bleat!"

"Then come home," said the boy. He led the goat into the stable and tied it up.

"Now then," said the tailor; "has the goat had its proper food?"

"Oh, yes," answered the son. "She is so full she hasn't room for another leaf."

The tailor didn't trust his word, and went again to the goat and asked, "Goat, are you really full?"

The wicked animal answered:

"How should I be full?
Grazing on the graves,
With not a leaf to eat?
Bleat! bleat!"

"Oh, you scamp!" exclaimed the tailor, "as bad and undutiful as your brothers. You shan't make a fool of me any longer"; and quite beside himself with anger, he thrashed the poor boy with the yard-measure so terribly that he ran away.

The old tailor was now left alone with the goat. The next morning he went to the stable, caressed the goat, and said, "Now, my pretty animal, I will myself take you out to graze." He put the cord round its neck, and led it to a hedge where there were nettles and other things goats like. "Eat to your heart's content," he said, and he let her graze till evening. Then he asked, "Goat, are you full?"

And she answered:

"I am so full,
Another leaf I could not eat,
Bleat! bleat!"

"Then come home," said the tailor, and led her into the stable and tied her up. As he was going away he turned round and said, "For once you are full."

But the goat called out as usual:

"How should I be full?
Grazing on the graves,
With not a leaf to eat?
Bleat! bleat!"

On hearing this the tailor knew the truth, and how he had turned out his three sons without just cause. "Wait a minute," he cried. "You ungrateful brute! to chase you away is not sufficient punishment; I will brand you first, so that you'll be ashamed to show yourself among honest tailors." He ran and fetched his razor, soaped the goat's head, then shaved it as smooth as his hand. And because the yard-measure seemed too honourable a weapon, he seized the whip instead, and lashed the goat till she bounded off in terror.

The tailor, all alone in his house, moped and fell into a melancholy condition. Gladly would he have had his sons back, but he had no idea what had become of them.

The eldest became apprenticed to a carpenter; he served his time diligently, and when his time was up, his master made him a present of a little table, which was made of ordinary wood, but had one peculiarity. If you put it down anywhere and said, "Little table, lay yourself," the good little table was at once covered with a clean cloth, a plate, knife and fork, dishes with boiled and roast meat, and a big bumper of red wine that did your heart good to look at, it sparkled so. The young fellow thought, "With this you will live in plenty all your life," and went to see the world, never troubling about whether an inn were good or bad. If it did not please him he didn't go in, but took his table into a wood or a meadow, or to any spot he fancied. Directly he put it down and said, "Lay yourself," everything was on it that his heart could desire.

At last it occurred to him to go back to his father, whose wrath by this time was sure to have died down, and who would welcome him if he came with the wonderful little table on his back.

It happened that while he was on the way he came to an inn that was filled with guests; they bade him welcome, and invited him to sit down with them to dinner, otherwise he would stand a poor chance of getting anything, as the inn was full.

"No," answered the carpenter, "I will not rob you of a mouthful—on the contrary, I should like to entertain you as my guests."

They laughed, and thought he was joking.

He, however, put down his wooden table in the middle of the room and said, " Little table, lay yourself." Immediately it was covered with good things to eat, far better than anything the host could supply, and the smell of which seemed very appetising to the guests.

" Set to work, dear friends," said the carpenter ; and the guests, when they saw he really meant it, did not wait to be asked again, but came to the table and plied their knives and forks with a will.

The host stood in a corner and looked on ; he didn't know at all what to make of it, but thought such a cook would be useful in his household.

The carpenter and the company he entertained were lively till midnight ; then they went to bed, and the young apprentice placed his table against the wall before he lay down to sleep. The host's thoughts were busy meanwhile, and he could not rest for thinking of an old table in the lumber-room that looked very much the same as this magic one. At last he went and brought it, and changed it with the carpenter's.

The next morning the carpenter paid his bill, packed up his dear table, little dreaming it was the wrong one, and went his way.

About midday he arrived at his father's, who received him with joyous greetings.

" My dear son, tell me what you've been doing," he said.

" Father, I have become a carpenter."

" A good trade ; but what have you brought away as a specimen of your craft ? "

" Father, the best thing I could bring was this table."

The tailor examined the table in every part, then said, " I can't say it is a masterpiece ; it strikes me as being a very old and a badly made table."

" But," said the son, " it is a table that lays itself ; I have only to place it somewhere and to tell it to lay itself, and it produces on the instant dainty dishes and delicious wine. Just invite all your friends and relatives to come and regale themselves ; the table will send them away well filled and happy."

When the company arrived, he placed the small table

in the middle of the room and said, "Little table, lay yourself," but the table did not stir, and remained as empty as any other table which did not understand language. Then the poor fellow discovered that the table had been changed, and hung his head in shame. The relatives laughed and made game of him, and they were obliged to take their way home unfed and without drinking anything. His father brought out his work again, and tailored away, and the poor son went to find employment in the service of a new master.

The second son meanwhile had gone as apprentice to a miller. When his year was up his master said, "You have worked and behaved so well, that I will give you a present of a donkey of a peculiar kind ; he cannot draw a cart or carry any sacks."

"What use is he, then ? " asked the young apprentice.

"He spits gold," answered the miller. "If you put him on a cloth and say, ' Bricklebrit,' the good animal will spit out gold coins before and behind."

"Good business," said the apprentice, thanked his master, and went out into the world. When he wanted money he had only to remark, "Bricklebrit" to his donkey, and there was a shower of gold coins ; so that he had no need to work for a living. Wherever he went he drew the line at nothing. The dearer things were the better, because his purse was always full.

After wandering for some time seeing the world he thought at last, "It's time you looked up your father again. If you return home with the gold donkey he will forget his anger and welcome you home."

Now it happened that on the way he put up at the same inn where his brother's table had been changed. He led his donkey by the hand, and his host wanted to take it from him and tie it up, but the young apprentice said, "Don't trouble, please ; I will take my grey steed myself into the stable and fasten him up, so that I shall know exactly where he is."

The host thought this curious, and was of opinion that a man who insisted on stabling his own donkey probably hadn't much to spend. However, when his guest put his hand in his pocket and, drawing forth two sovereigns, asked him to bring in a supply of good fare, he opened his eyes with surprise, then ran and procured the best that was to be had.

After the meal the stranger asked how much he had still to pay, and the host, to make as much out of him as possible, said, " Two sovereigns more."

The apprentice put his hand in his pocket, but found his supply of gold had run out. " Wait a minute, landlord," he said, " I will go and fetch more money," and he took the tablecloth with him. The host's curiosity was aroused, and he followed on tiptoe. The guest bolted the stable door behind him, but the spy looked through the keyhole and saw him spread the cloth under the donkey. Directly he had exclaimed " Bricklebrit," the animal begun to spit gold from every part, till the ground was covered.

" Ah, by Jove ! " said the host, " in that way sovereigns are quickly coined ! I wouldn't mind possessing such a mint."

The guest paid his bill and retired to bed.

In the night the host sneaked out to his stable, removed the money-making donkey, and put an ordinary donkey in its place.

Early the following morning the apprentice set off with the animal, which he thought was his gold donkey, arriving at noon at his father's house. He received a warm welcome.

" What have you been doing all this time, son ? " asked the old man.

" I have learnt to be a miller," he answered.

" And what have you brought as a specimen of your labours ? "

" Nothing but a donkey."

" Donkeys are common enough here," said his father. ' I would rather it had been a good goat."

" Yes," answered the son, " but this is no common donkey ; you have only to say, ' Bricklebrit,' and the animal will spit out for you a cloth full of sovereigns. Invite all the relatives we have to come and make their fortunes."

" That will be greatly to my mind," said the tailor, " and I needn't slave at my needle any longer."

So when all the relatives had come the young miller told

them to sit down, and he spread out the cloth and brought the donkey into the room. "Now look out," he said, and shouted "Bricklebrit," but no gold coins appeared, and it was evident the donkey had no notion of the art of producing them. Not every donkey is so clever.

The poor miller pulled a long face and begged the relatives' pardon. They had to go home as poor as they came ; and the poor old man was obliged to drudge with his needle as he had always done, while the youth took a place under another miller.

The third brother had gone to a turner's to learn the trade, and because turning is an artistic calling, his was the longest apprenticeship. His brothers wrote and told him the misfortunes which had befallen them, and how the host of the inn at which they had put up had stolen their valuable magic gifts.

Now when the turner had learnt all there was to learn of the business, and was going to travel, his master presented him with a sack, and remarked, "There is a cudgel inside."

"The sack I can rest on ; but what good is the cudgel ? It will only make the sack heavy."

"Listen," said the master. "If anyone threatens you, all you've to say is, ' Cudgel, jump out of the sack,' and the cudgel will jump out, and will dance on the backs of people so effectively that they will have to lie still and not move for ten days afterwards."

The apprentice thanked him, slung the sack over his shoulder, and whenever anybody came too near, or was in any way offensive, he merely said, "Cudgel, jump out of the sack," and the cudgel came out and laid about with a will on the backs of the rascals.

The young turner came one evening to the same inn where his brothers had been swindled. He laid his wares on the table, and began to relate stories of the wonderful things he had seen on his travels. "Yes," he said, "it's all very well to talk about tables that cover themselves, and donkeys that coin sovereigns, but I have a treasure in my sack compared with which these things are nothing at all."

The host pricked up his ears and thought, "The sack is

full of precious stones, I'll be bound. I'll get it cheaply ; all good things come in threes."

When it was time to retire the turner stretched himself on a form, using the sack as a pillow. The host, thinking the guest was in a deep slumber, crept up and began looking at the sack to see if he could pull it from under the sleeper's head and exchange it for another.

The turner, however, had long been on the look-out, and just as the host had made up his mind to give him a shove and take the sack, he cried, " Cudgel, come out ! " Immediately the cudgel jumped forth on to the host's body, which he first scraped, according to a little custom of his, and then began to flog.

The host screamed for mercy, but all the lustier was the cudgel in beating time on his back, till at last the victim fell exhausted on the floor.

The turner then said, " If you will not restore to me the magic table and the gold donkey of which you robbed my brothers, the dance shall begin all over again."

" Ah, no, please," cried the host in a faint voice. " I will restore everything if you will only tell this wretched thing to get back in the sack."

" I will be gracious and show mercy, now justice has been done," said the turner, " but take care what you do next." He then called out, " Cudgel, jump into the sack, and let the host alone."

The next morning the turner set out, taking with him the magic table and the gold donkey. When he arrived at his father's the old tailor was delighted to see him, and asked what he had learnt while he had been out in the world.

" Dear father," he answered, " I have learnt to be a turner."

" A very artistic trade," remarked the father. " And what have you to show ? "

" A most costly article, dear father," replied the son, " a cudgel in a sack."

" What ! " exclaimed his father, " a cudgel ! You can cut one from any tree you come to."

" But not one like this, dear father. If I say, ' Cudgel, jump out of the sack,' the cudgel jumps out, and leads anyone who is not friendly to me a dance, beating him till he lies on the ground crying for mercy. Look, with this cudgel I have got back the table that spread itself, and a gold donkey, which a rascally cheating landlord stole from my brothers. Now summon all our relatives and friends and let them eat and drink, and fill their pockets with gold sovereigns."

The old tailor looked rather unbelieving, but sent for the relatives.

Then the turner fetched a cloth and led in the gold donkey. He said to his brother, " Now, my dear boy, speak to him."

The miller said, " Bricklebrit," and on the instant gold coins rained into the cloth, and the donkey did not stop till everyone had picked up more than he could carry. (Don't you wish you had been there ?) Next the turner fetched the table and said to the other brother, " Speak to it, dear brother." Scarcely had the carpenter cried, " Little table, spread yourself," than it was covered with the most delicious things to eat. A meal was eaten the like of which had never been known in the tailor's house before, and the relatives remained till late, and were all merry and contented.

The tailor for the future locked up his needle and thread, his yard-measure, and his iron, in a cupboard, and lived at his ease with his three sons in comfort and plenty.

What, however, had become of the goat, who had been the cause of the tailor turning his sons out into the world ? I will tell you. She was so ashamed of her shaven, bald head, that she hid herself in a fox's hole, and when the fox came home he saw a pair of great eyes glowering at him out of the darkness, and was so alarmed that he retreated.

The bear met him, and, noticing his disturbed appearance, asked, " What ails you, brother Fox ? Why do you make that anxious face ? "

" Oh," answered Rufus, " a horrible creature is sitting in my hole with great fiery, glaring eyes."

" Come, we will drive it out together," said the bear, and went to the hole and looked in. When, however, he saw the fiery eyes, he, too, was seized with fear, and declined to have anything to do with the terrible creature.

As he turned away he met a bee, and seeing something bad had upset him she said, " Bear, what a distressed face ! Why are you in such low spirits ? "

"You may well ask," answered the bear. " A horrible creature is sitting in my friend Rufus's house, and we cannot drive it out."

The bee answered, " Poor weak little thing that I am, I believe I can help you." And she flew into the fox's hole, stung the goat on its bald head over and over again, till with a bleat ! bleat ! it sprang out and ran away.

M

The Three Golden Hairs

THERE was once a poor woman who had a son, of whom it was foretold that in his fourteenth year he should marry the king's daughter.

At the time of his birth it happened that the king passed through the village unknown to anyone, and as he asked the news he was told that a child had just been born, and that it had been foretold that everything this child undertook would succeed, and that he would marry the king's daughter when he was fourteen years old.

The king had a bad heart, and this prediction made him angry. He went to see the parents of the child, and said in a friendly way, " You are poor people ; give me your child, I will take care of it."

They refused at first, but the stranger offered them gold, and they said to each other, " As the child is born lucky, whatever happens will turn out well for him." So at last they consented to part with their son.

The king put the child into a box and went down with his burden to the bank of a steep river, into which he threw it, thinking thus to rid his daughter of a suitor whom she hardly expected. But the box, instead of sinking, floated like a little boat, and not a drop of water found its way in. It floated down the stream till within two miles of the capital, and was stopped by the flood-gate of a mill. A miller's boy who happened to be there saw it, and pulled it towards him with a crook. He opened it, expecting to find great treasure, but it was only a pretty little boy, brisk and handsome. He carried him to the mill ; the miller and his wife, who had no children of their own, received this little one as if Heaven had sent him. They treated the orphan in the best possible way, and he stayed with them, and grew up hearty and strong and clever.

One day the king, surprised by rain, entered the mill for shelter, and asked the miller if this tall youth were his son.

"No, your Majesty," replied the miller; "he is a foundling who came to our mill-dam in a box, fourteen years ago; our mill boy took him out of the water."

Then the king knew it was the child he had thrown into the river.

"Good people," said he, "could this youngster carry a letter from me to the queen? I would give him two pieces of gold for his pains."

"As your Majesty pleases," replied they, and told the young man to be ready.

The king wrote a letter to the queen, in which he told her to have the messenger put to death, and buried, so that he might find the thing done when he came home.

The youth set out with the letter, but lost his way, and at night found himself in the midst of a great forest. Through the darkness he descried in the distance a feeble light, and, making his way in that direction, he came to a little hut, where he saw an old woman sitting before the fire. She seemed surprised to see the young man, and asked, "Whence come you, and what do you want?"

"I come from the mill," he replied. "I am carrying a letter to the queen. I've lost my way, and should be glad to pass the night here."

"Unhappy youth," replied the woman, "you've fallen into a den of robbers; if they find you your doom is sealed."

"With Heaven's protection I am not afraid," said the youth. "Moreover, I am so tired that I could not possibly travel further."

He laid himself down on a bench and went to sleep. The robbers came in soon afterwards, and angrily asked why the stranger was there. "Oh," said the old woman, "he is a poor boy who has lost his way in the wood, and I took him in out of compassion. He is carrying a letter to the queen."

The robbers took the letter and saw that it directed the queen to have the messenger put to death. In spite of the hardness of their hearts, they felt compassion towards the poor young fellow; and their captain tore the letter up and substituted another for it, directing that as soon as the youth arrived he should immediately marry the king's daughter. Then the robbers let him sleep on his bench till morning, and when he awoke they gave him the letter and showed him his way.

The queen, when she received the letter, fulfilled the behests therein. A splendid wedding was held. The king's daughter married the lucky youth; and as he was a handsome, good-natured young fellow, she was glad to live with him.

Some time afterwards the king came home to his palace to find the prediction accomplished, and the lucky youth married to his daughter.

"How has this happened?" said he. "I had given very different injunctions in my letter."

The queen showed him the letter that he might see the contents. He read it, and saw that his own letter had been taken away. He asked the young man what had become of the letter entrusted to him, and why he had delivered another instead.

"I know nothing about it," said the youth. "It must have been changed during the night while I was asleep in the forest."

The king said to him in anger, "This shall not pass thus. He who aspires to my daughter's hand must bring me from the underground cave three golden hairs from the Great Ogre's head. Bring these and my daughter shall be yours."

The king said this in hope that he would never return from such a mission.

The young man replied, "I am not afraid of the Ogre. I'll go and seek the three golden hairs." And he took leave of the king and set out on his journey.

He came to a great town. At the gate the sentinel asked him what was his trade and what he knew.

"Everything," he replied.

"Then," said the sentinel, "do us the favour to tell us why the fountain of our market-place, which used to run with wine, does not even give us water, but is dried up."

"Wait," said he, "I'll tell you on my return."

Farther on he came to another town. The sentinel at the gate asked who he was and what he knew.

"Everything," he replied.

"Then do us the favour to inform us why the great tree of our town, which used to bear golden apples, has now not even leaves."

"Wait," said he ; "I'll tell you on my return."

Farther on he came to a great river, which he had to cross. The ferryman asked him who he was and what he knew.

"Everything," replied he.

"Then," said the ferryman, "do me the kindness to inform me whether I am always to stay at this post and never be relieved."

"Stop," he replied ; I'll tell you on my return."

On the further side of the water he found the entrance to the Ogre's cave. It was very black and smoky. The Ogre was not at home ; there was only his housekeeper, sitting in a large arm-chair.

"What do you want?" she asked, in a sufficiently friendly voice.

"I want three golden hairs from the Ogre's head, for without them I cannot have my wife."

"That's asking a great deal," she replied ; "if the Ogre were to see you when he comes in you'd have a bad time. But I like your looks, and will see what is to be done."

She changed him into an ant, and said, "Hide yourself in the folds of my dress ; you'll be in safety there."

"Thank you," he said, "that will do famously. But I also want to know three things. Why does a fountain which used to run with wine not even yield water now? Why does a tree which used to give golden apples not even bear leaves? And is a certain ferryman always to remain at his post without ever being relieved?"

"Those are three difficult questions," she observed. "But be very quiet, and pay attention to what the Ogre says when I pull out his three golden hairs."

In the evening the Ogre came home. As soon as he entered he noticed an extraordinary smell. "There's something strange here," he said, "I smell man's flesh."

And he grubbed about in all the corners without finding anything.

The housekeeper began finding fault with him. "I've just been sweeping and arranging the place," said she, "and you put everything in disorder. You're always fancying you smell human flesh ; sit down and eat your supper."

When he had supped he was tired ; he laid his head on his housekeeper's knees, and told her to scratch his head for him ; and he soon began to sleep and snore. Then the old woman seized a golden hair, pulled it out and put it aside.

"Ha !" cried the Ogre, "what are you about ? "

"I had a bad dream," she replied, "and that made me catch you by the hair."

"What did you dream ? " he asked.

"I dreamed that the fountain in a market-place which used to pour forth wine had stopped, and would not even give water ; what can be the reason ? "

"Ah ! if they knew that ! " replied the Ogre, "there's a toad under a stone in the fountain ; if they would only kill that, the wine would begin to flow again."

The housekeeper began to rub his head again ; and he went to sleep and snored in such a manner that all the windows shook. Then she tore a second hair from his head. "Ho ! what are you about ? " cried the Ogre, angrily.

"Don't put yourself out," she replied, "it's only a dream I had."

"What have you been dreaming about ? " he asked.

"I dreamed that in a country there was a tree which always bore golden apples, and that now it has not even leaves. What can be the reason of that ? "

"Ah ! if they only knew ! " cried the Ogre. "There's a mouse gnawing the root. If they only killed it, the tree would bear apples again ; but if the mouse goes on gnawing it the tree will die altogether. Now leave me in peace with your dreams, and if you disturb me again, I'll give you a box on the ear."

The housekeeper quieted him and began to rub his head again, till he was asleep and snoring. Then she seized the third golden hair and pulled it out. The Ogre rose with a shout and was going to beat her, but she softened him again by saying, " Who can help having a bad dream ? "

" And what have you been dreaming now ? " he asked, curiously.

" I dreamed that a ferryman was complaining that he was always keeping the ferry with his boat, and that no one ever came to relieve him."

" Ho, the foolish fellow," exclaimed the Ogre, " he's only to put his oar into the hands of the first man who comes to pass the river and then he'll be free, and the other will be obliged to act as ferryman in his turn."

As the housekeeper had now pulled out the three golden hairs, and extracted the three answers from the Ogre, she left him in peace, and he slept till the morning.

When the Ogre had left the house the old lady took the hairs out from the folds of her gown, and restored the young man to his own shape. " There are three hairs," said she, " but did you hear the answers the Ogre gave to your questions ? "

" Very well," replied he, " and I shall remember them."

" Then your turn is served," said she, " and you can set out on your journey."

He thanked the old lady who had given him such kind help, and went out of the smoky cave, very glad at having succeeded so well.

When he came to the ferry he caused the man to put him across before he told him the answer the Ogre had taught him. Then he said, " You have only to put your oar into the hand of the first man who comes to pass the river."

Further on he came to the town of the sterile tree. The sentinel was also waiting for his answer. " Kill the mouse that is gnawing the root," said he, " and the golden apples will grow again."

The sentinel, to reward him, gave him two asses laden with gold.

At last he came to the city where the fountain was dry. He said to the sentinel, " There's a toad under a stone in the fountain ; look for it and kill it, and the wine will begin to flow again abundantly."

The sentinel thanked him, and also gave him two asses laden with gold.

At last the lucky youth came to his wife, who rejoiced heartily to see him return, and to hear that all had turned out well. He gave the Ogre's three golden hairs to the king.

The king was highly satisfied when he saw the four asses laden with gold, and said to him, " Now all the conditions are fulfilled, and my daughter is yours. But tell me, my dear son-in-law, how you come by so much gold ? For that's an immense treasure you bring back."

" I found it," said he, " on the banks of a certain river I crossed. It's the sand of the shore there."

" Could I get as much for myself ? " asked the king, who was a miser.

" As much as you like," he replied, " you'll find a ferry-man, apply to him to pass the river, and you may fill your sacks."

The covetous monarch immediately set out, and when he came to the river, made signs to the ferryman to bring over his boat. The ferryman took him across, and when they were at the other side, put his oar into the king's hand and jumped out. Thus the king became a ferryman as a punishment for his sins.

" And is he there still ? "

" Certainly ; for nobody has taken the oar from him."

The True Bride

THERE was once a young and beautiful maiden. She had lost her mother when a child, and her stepmother did everything she could to make her life a burden. When she gave her any work, however difficult it might be, the girl went at it untiringly, and did as much as was in her power. But she was unable to touch the wicked woman's heart in this way; she was never satisfied, and always found the girl had not done enough; in fact, the harder she worked the more she was given to do; and the only way she got thanked was by being burdened with heavier loads, and by her life being made utterly miserable.

One day her stepmother said to her, " There are twelve pounds of feathers for you to pluck, and if you have not finished by this evening you may expect a good beating. Do you imagine you can sit idle all day ? "

The poor girl set to work, but the tears poured down her cheeks, for she saw it was impossible for her to finish the work in a day. If, in her distress, she sighed, or wrung her hands together, when a little pile of feathers were lying before her they flew apart, and she had to pick them up again and start afresh. At last she put her elbows on the table, hid her face in her hands, and cried out, " Is there no one on God's earth to have pity on me ? " Whereupon she heard a soft voice, saying, " Be comforted, my child, I have come to help you."

The girl looked up, and saw an old woman standing by her side. She took the girl kindly by the hand, and said, " Confide your troubles in me."

She spoke so gently that the girl told her all about her sad life, and explained how burden upon burden was laid upon her, and how impossible it was for her to get through her present work. " If I have not done these feathers by this evening my stepmother will beat me; she has threatened me with it, and she always keeps her word;" The girl began to cry again, but the old woman said: "Never mind, child, go and rest yourself, and in the meantime I will do your work for you."

The girl lay down on her bed, and was soon fast asleep. The old woman sat down at the table with the feathers, and oh! how they flew off the quills, which she scarcely touched with her hard hands. She soon finished the twelve pounds.

When the girl awoke large snow-white heaps of feathers were lying piled up, and the room was cleanly swept out, but the old woman had vanished. The girl thanked God, and remained quiet until evening.

When her stepmother came in she was simply astonished to find the work completed. "You see, you lazy thing," said she, "what can be done if one is diligent. Could you not have found something else to do instead of sitting there with your hands in your lap?"

As she was leaving the room she said to herself, "That creature is worth more than her salt. I must give her some harder work to do."

The next morning she called the girl and said, "Here is a spoon, go and clear out the big pond at the bottom of the garden with it, and if you have not finished by this evening you know what will follow."

The girl took the spoon and saw that it had a hole in it; but even if this had not been the case she could never have emptied the pond with it. However, she set to work at once, and kneeling beside the water, into which her tears fell, began to bale.

But the good old woman appeared again, and when she learnt the cause of the girl's distress, said, "Be comforted, my child; go and sleep in the bushes, and I will do your work for you."

When she was alone, the old woman merely touched the water and it began to rise into the air like vapour and mingle with the clouds.

Gradually the pond became empty, and when at sunset the girl awoke there was nothing to be seen but the fishes flapping in the mud. She went to her stepmother and showed her that the work was completed.

" You ought to have finished long ago," she said, turning white with rage, and already beginning to turn over in her mind what she could now give the girl to do.

The third morning she said to her, " You are to build a beautiful castle for me on that piece of level ground over there, and it must be ready by this evening."

The poor girl was utterly dismayed, and said, " How could I ever execute such a great piece of work ? "

" I will stand no contradiction," screamed her step-mother. " If you can empty out a pond with a spoon with a hole in it, you can build a castle. I shall take up my abode there to-day, and if there is anything missing, even if it be the most trifling thing in the kitchen or cellar, you know what to expect," and she drove the girl away.

When the latter reached the valley she found rocks piled up one against the other ; using all her strength, she could not even move the smallest of them.

She sat down and began to cry, her one hope lying in the appearance of the old woman, who did not keep her waiting long, but came and comforted her by saying, " Just lie down and sleep in the shade, and I will build your castle for you, and if it pleases you, you shall live in it yourself."

When the girl was gone the old woman touched the grey rocks. Immediately they began to move towards each other, and stood side by side as if a giant had built the wall ; then the building began to form, and it was just as if innumerable unseen hands were working and laying stone upon stone. The earth groaned, and great pillars arose and arranged themselves in order, the tiles placed themselves neatly on the roof, and at midday a weathercock, like a golden virgin with flying garments, was turning on the top of the tower. The inside of the castle was completed by the evening. How the old woman managed it I really do not know, but the walls of the rooms were hung with silk and velvet, richly upholstered chairs were standing about, handsomely carved arm-chairs were placed in front of marble tables, and crystal chandeliers hung from the ceiling and were reflected in the polished floor. Green parrots and beautiful singing birds were swinging in gold cages, and everywhere was splendour worthy of a king.

The sun was just setting when the girl awoke and found thousands of lights flashing in her eyes. She got up quickly and ran into the castle through the open door. The steps were covered with red cloth, and the golden railings garnished with flowering trees. When she beheld the splendour of the rooms she stood still, absolutely stupefied. Who knows how long she would have remained so, if she had not suddenly remembered her stepmother. " Ah ! " she said to herself, " if only she could be satisfied at last, and not frighten me out of my wits any longer." So the maiden went and told her mother that the castle was ready.

" I will go and inhabit it at once," she said, getting up from her seat.

When she entered the castle she had to put her hands before her eyes, the brilliancy dazzled her so. " You see," she said to the girl, " how easily you do everything. I ought to have given you something more difficult." She went through all the rooms and poked into every corner, to see if anything were missing or wrong, but could find nothing.

" Now we will go below," she said, casting a look of hatred at the girl. " The kitchen and cellars have yet to be looked through, and if you have forgotten anything you shall not escape your punishment."

But the fire was burning on the hearth, and the supper cooking in the pots, the shovel and tongs were in their place, a row of shining kitchen utensils arranged against the wall. Nothing was missing, not even the coal-box or the water-pail.

" Where is the entrance to the cellar ? " she cried. " If it is not well filled with wine it will be a bad thing for you." She lifted up the trap-door herself and went down the steps, but she had scarcely taken two steps before the heavy trap-door, which was only tilted back, fell on her. The girl heard a cry and quickly lifted the trap-door to help her, but it had knocked her down, and she lay lifeless at the bottom.

Now the beautiful castle belonged to the girl alone. At first she did not know what to do, she was so happy; the cupboards were filled with beautiful clothes, and some of the drawers with gold and silver, and others with pearls and precious stones; in fact, she had everything she wanted.

Soon the renown of the girl's beauty and riches went throughout the world. Suitors presented themselves daily, but none pleased her. At last a king's son came, and he succeeded in winning her heart, and they were engaged.

In the castle gardens was a lime-tree, under which the lovers were one day sitting happily together, when he said to her, " I must go home and get my father's permission for our marriage. I beseech you to wait for me here, under this tree, and I shall be back in a few hours."

The girl kissed him on his left cheek and said, " Keep true to me, and don't let anyone kiss you on this cheek. I will wait for you under this lime-tree."

She sat on under the lime-tree until sunset, but he had not returned. She sat there for three entire days and waited for him, but in vain.

When he did not appear on the fourth day she said, " Something most certainly must have happened to him, I will go and look for him, and not come back until I have found him." She packed up her three prettiest dresses, one covered with shining stars, the second with silver moons, and the third with golden suns, and also a handful of precious stones, and set out. Everywhere she went she inquired after her lover, but no one had either seen or heard of him. She wandered far and wide over the world, but could not find him. At last she hired herself out to a farmer as a shepherdess, and hid her dresses and precious stones under a large rock.

She now lived as a shepherdess, and while tending her sheep was very sad, longing for her beloved. She had a little calf, which grew quite tame, and used to eat out of her hand, and when she said:

> " Kneel down, little calf, by my side,
>   Come closer unto me ;
> Be not as the prince who forgot his bride
>   Under the old lime-tree,"

the calf knelt down and let her stroke it.

After having thus spent two sad and lonely years, the news that the king's daughter was going to be married was spread over the land. The road to the town passed through the village where the maiden was living, and it happened that once while she was tending her sheep the bridegroom passed by. He sat proudly on his horse, and did not look near her, but she saw him and recognised her lover. She felt as if a sharp knife were cutting her heart. " Ah ! " she sighed, " I thought he would have remained true to me, but he has forgotten."

Another day he passed along the road. When he came near she said to the calf :

> " Kneel down, little calf, by my side,
>   Come closer unto me;
>   Be not as the prince who forgot his bride
>   Under the old lime-tree."

When he heard the voice he looked round, and reined in his horse. He looked the shepherdess in the face, and put his hands to his eyes as if he wanted to remember something, then rode on farther, and soon disappeared.

" Alas ! " she cried, " he does not know me any longer," and she was sadder than ever.

Soon afterwards the whole country was invited to a three days' feast given by the king at his court. " Now," thought she, " I will try my last chance."

When evening came she went to the rock, took out the dress covered with golden suns, put it on, and adorned herself with precious stones. She unbound her hair, which she had been wearing concealed under a handkerchief, and let her long curls fall down her back. She then went to the town, and as it was dark no one noticed her. At her appearance in the brilliantly lighted hall everybody started in astonishment, but nobody knew who she was. The prince went forward to meet her, but still he did not recognise her. He danced with her, and was so charmed with her beauty that he scarcely gave the other bride a thought. When the *fête* was over she disappeared in the crowd, and was back in the village before break of day, clad once more in her shepherdess dress.

The next evening she wore her dress with the moons, and put a crescent moon of precious stones in her hair. When she appeared at the banquet everyone turned to gaze at her, but the king's son hastened towards her, danced with her the whole evening, and would not look at anyone else. Before she went away he made her promise that she would come again the next evening.

When she appeared the third evening she was wearing the star dress, which shimmered and glittered at every step she took, and in her hair and round her waist were stars of precious stones.

The prince had been waiting for her a long time, and managed to press his way towards her. When he reached her he said, " Now, do tell me who you are. It seems to me I have known you for a long time."

" Don't you remember what I did when we parted ? " she answered, and, stepping up to him, kissed his left cheek.

At that moment scales seemed to fall from his eyes, and he recognised his true bride. " Come away," he said, " I cannot stay here any longer," and, seizing her hand, he led her to the carriage.

The horses seemed to fly like the wind to the magic castle, and they could see the illuminated windows shining from afar. On passing the lime-tree it shook its branches and sent a sweet fragrance into the air ; underneath it were an innumerable quantity of glow-worms. Flowers adorned the steps, and the song of the birds echoed in the rooms, but in the hall the whole court had assembled, and a priest was there waiting to unite the bridegroom to his true bride.